The Enchanted Hollow

To Ayra,
Enjoy!

The Enchanted Hollow

Written & Illustrated By

E.A. Olsen

Table of Contents

Ch.1..... The Hollow at Boggy Creek.

Ch.2..... Caroline comes to Boggy Creek.

Ch.3..... A day on the River.

Ch.4..... A Voyage with the Captain.

Ch.5..... The Big Thunderstorm and what it brought.

Ch.6..... Trent meets Lucifer.

Ch.7..... The Hollow works its magic.

Ch.8 .....A Trip to The City.

Ch.9.....Caroline has a Surprise.

Dedicated with love to my mother,
Nikki Scheuer, who has always made
me believe I can do anything.

Chapter One

The Hollow at Boggy Creek.

The bell above the glass door jangled merrily when Freddie Thompson entered Mr. Sweete's old fashioned Drugstore and Soda Fountain.

Freddie was a lean woman with long hair kept in a pony tail. She always wore soft old tee shirts, often with more than one hole, cutoff shorts and a faded baseball cap with a horse embroidered on the front.

Beside her strode two very tall dogs with long, silky hair. They were Russian Wolfhounds, or Borzois as they were called in their native country. Borzoi means swift and agile in Russian. One was red with golden feathers on his tail and legs. His name was Pirate. The other was stout and black as India ink. His snowy white chest made him look as if he wore a tuxedo. He was The King.

Freddie took a seat at the counter. The dogs sat down politely next to her.

Mr. Sweete had a warm smile for all three of them. "Good to see you, Miss Freddie," he said. "Can I get you a milkshake and maybe something for you boys?"

When he said "boys" he really meant the two dogs.

"Just iced tea for me," Freddie replied. "It's an oven out there." She wiped her sweaty forehead with a paper napkin.

The King growled softly. "What about us?"

Mr. Sweete grinned. "A scoop of vanilla for you two, perhaps?"

Pirate and The King both wagged their tails. They cleaned their bowls with dispatch and licked the rims until they shined.

"So how is the Captain faring?" Mr. Sweete asked. The Captain was Freddie's boyfriend.

"He's very happy. It's been a terrific year for tuna. I expect him back later this week." Freddie smiled as she spoke.

Before they could say more, the bell jingled again. A very plump, rather old lady with hair an improbable shade of light blue, came in. Tucked under one sausage like arm was a white, fluffy poodle with tiny blue bows on its ears.

"Good day, Miss Emmeline. Good day, Mitzi." Freddie greeted both woman and dog.

Pirate and The King barked their greeting to Mitzi.

The poodle yapped in a demanding tone. "Let me down. Let me down I say!" Mitzi wriggled in her owner's firm grasp.

But Miss Emmeline was deaf to the little dog's cries. "Whatever is the matter with you, Mitzi? She can be so difficult," complained the elderly lady.

"Why don't you ask Freddie?" Mr. Sweete advised, though he knew Miss Emmeline would never believe Freddie could truly speak with animals. Mr. Sweete knew Freddie did. He had never grown up on the inside, no matter what his gray whiskers proclaimed. The magic in his heart still beat true.

Miss Emmeline Harridan was another story all together. "Don't be absurd, Horace Sweete. Now stop that, Mitzi!" She shifted the struggling dog so she had a more secure grip.

"Why don't you let her down," Freddie suggested, undismayed by Miss Emmeline's skepticism. "The King and Pirate are dying to say hello."

"Dying to eat her more likely. Look at the snarls on their faces."

Pirate and The King were showing an excessive amount of teeth but they were smiling not snarling at the dainty little girl dog.

Freddie hid her grin. "I shouldn't think they're hungry. They've just had ice cream."

Suddenly, Mitzi twisted and slipped out of Miss Emmeline's arms. The poodle jumped to the floor and pranced coyly over to the handsome male dogs.

"I can't bear to watch!" Miss Emmeline declared dramatically and covered her eyes.

The King touched noses with Mitzi. "The bows are very fetching," he complimented her. The poodle bridled with pleasure. Pirate licked her ear with slavish devotion.

"You can look, Miss Emmeline." Freddie said dryly. "I think she'll survive the encounter."

"Will you stop carrying on, Emmeline." Mr. Sweete said sternly. "That little mop of yours is fine."

Miss Emmeline ignored him as she tried to recapture Mitzi. The nimble poodle skipped out of reach.

Mr. Sweete and Freddie choked as they tried not to laugh at the rotund Miss Emmeline scurry after Mitzi.

With a wild lunge, that nearly tipped her over, Miss Emmeline grabbed Mitzi. She glared at the gasping twosome with annoyance. "Like a pack of jackals, you are. Well, I'll be leaving then." Miss Emmeline swept out with all the dignity she could muster, since her straw hat was now badly askew. Mitzi tucked once again beneath her arm.

"Her rheumatism must be acting up." Mr. Sweete commented, "Emmeline is usually better humored."

"I'll drop off some more of my special poultice. John Henry swears by it." Freddie made a mental note to stop by Miss Emmeline's farm the next day. "I must be getting back to The Hollow. Have a nice afternoon, Mr. Sweete."

"You too, Miss Freddie. I'll be coming down to visit you one of these days soon."

"Please do. We always enjoy congenial company down at The Hollow." Freddie's step was now brisk as she hurried out to catch a ride home with John Henry. It was not beyond him to grow impatient and leave her to walk.

Early the next morning, the sun's bright shafts darted through the branches of the pine trees, and peeked into the windows of the cottage at The Hollow. The many creatures of the house began to wake, both two and four legged, to enjoy the few hours before the hot Southern summer drove them back into the cool of the shade.

Throw rugs scattered about the rooms rose, and took shape as tall, elegant Russian Wolfhounds. One by one, they let themselves out the front door. A cream and silver tabby cat stretched, then began her morning ablutions on the bed. She carefully licked between each toe. Freddie sat up amongst rumpled covers.

"Good Morning, Esmerelda," she said to the cat.

The cat paused in her washing, her green eyes blinked slowly.

"Good Morning, Freddie." Esmerelda answered. "The dogs left all in a flurry this morning. Change is coming, can you taste it?"

Freddie, whose real name was Fredricka though she never used it, went to stand in the sun by the window. The light made her hair shine copper as a new penny.

"I feel it, too."

"Maybe Captain Jeff is coming for a visit." The cat offered.

Freddie frowned, considering. "No, it feels different than that. Someone younger. A girl. I can't imagine who though."

Freddie went into the kitchen and brewed a pot of strong coffee. Esmerelda jumped on the counter and daintily helped herself to a few bites of kibble.

The King strolled into the kitchen. He sat down in a stately manner and nodded politely to the cat, who nodded back.

"You're needed up at the road, Freddie. The Mailman is looking for the driveway again."

"Thank you, King. One of these days I'm going to have to convince those Crape Myrtle bushes that we needn't be hidden from everyone."

"Those shrubs are too dense to learn anything new." The dog chuckled at his pun.

Freddie left the house, curious. It had to be something important. No one came to The Hollow otherwise, and they'd picked up the mail only yesterday.

When she reached the end of the drive, the bushes parted for her and revealed a slightly confused Mailman.

"Howdy, Miss Freddie. Can't ever seem to find your driveway until all of a sudden it's right under my nose. Got an Over Night Letter for you."

"Thank you, Bob." Freddie took the envelope. The return address was Camp Meadowlark up in Virginia. How odd, she thought. "Would you like a cup of coffee? It's fresh brewed."

"I wish I could. Too many deliveries to make." Bob said reluctantly. A visit to Freddie's tree house with her pets was always a pleasure. Even if it was a little eerie how her critters seemed to understand her. "You have a nice day now."

Freddie went back to the cottage and tore open the envelope. It was from the Head of Camp Meadowlark and read:

Dear Miss Fredricka Thompson,

Your niece Caroline is a camper here at Meadowlark. Your brother and his wife were lost in a storm while ballooning across the Atlantic. They have not been heard from since. The July session has come to a close and you are named as Guardian. Please advise as to when you can come fetch Caroline.

Sincerely, Miss Cram

Head of Camp Meadowlark

Terribly concerned, Freddie stepped outside and filled the birdbath. When the water calmed, still as a mirror, she gazed into the reflection and concentrated on her older brother, Matthew and his allergy prone wife, Sarah, who were lost ballooning.

When they weren't ballooning, Sarah was a Doctor who treated allergies. She herself had such severe allergies she sneezed almost all the time. Matthew worked for the Government in a high placed position. Sarah loved to balloon high above the ground, away from the pollens that made her eyes water and her nose run. Matthew did not have allergies but he loved to balloon anyway.

Freddie hadn't seen them in years. The Doctor had been sick and miserable the one time they visited The Hollow. Freddie suspected the Doctor believed she, Freddie, was crazy. Freddie thought the Doctor rather a nuisance. Freddie, like many people without allergies, was impatient with those who did have them.

Freddie drew on the magic of The Hollow, searching for her missing brother. But the vision in the birdbath remained cloudy. They were too far away for the magic to reach. She worried about their whereabouts but there was nothing more she could do.

Esmerelda rubbed herself against Freddie's legs. "They'll be fine you know." The cat's voice was reassuring.

"I'm sure you're right, kitten. I'd feel it, if they were truly in trouble."

Freddie scratched her head. She had never met her niece, though she had a photo of the petite girl with straight, black hair and eyes as dark as midnight. Caroline was eleven, that was certainly old enough to travel by herself. It was impossible for Freddie to leave The Hollow right now. Only she and Captain Jeff could enter freely and the Captain was far out in the Gulf waters this week. That was the problem with magic, sometimes it was inconvenient. Caroline would be just fine on her own, she decided.

At the old fashioned kitchen table, she composed the answering telegram:

To the Head of Camp Meadowlark, stop, (They always use stop instead of periods in telegrams) Please send Caroline on the train to Boggy Creek tomorrow, stop, I will pick her up at the station, stop, Thank you, stop, Fredricka Thompson, stop.

Satisfied with her message she went back outside. Her dogs gathered around her, their dark eyes sparkled with curiosity. Silky coated Wolfhounds in every color, black, red, spotted and brown, waved their plumy tails. A chestnut horse, with four white stockings and a blaze, gleamed copper. His ears pricked hard forward and he pawed with one hoof impatiently.

"Well, are you going to tell us the news, Freddie? These fool dogs of yours have been running wild all morning."

"We are going to have a visitor, John Henry. In fact, I need a volunteer to take my telegram to town."

"I'll go. I'll go." Tess and Speed barked excitedly. They were black and tan, and black and white, in that order.

Freddie shook her head. Within the magic confines of The Hollow they behaved relatively well, but they were young and needed supervision. High on their list of fun things to do was scaring the town cats half to death.

"Sorry, not this time. Pirate, how about you?"

The dog's long, red-gold hair fluttered in the breeze. "I'll go, if John Henry goes." He growled shrewdly.

Freddie knew she was in for some bargaining. John Henry never did anything for nothing. Not even things he enjoyed, like visiting in town.

John Henry looked bored and yawned hugely, his bargaining face.

"A half scoop extra of grain." Freddie offered.

The horse snorted haughtily. "Two at the very least."

"One or I go in with you and run errands all day."

"Heaven forbid, it'll be too hot for that. One scoop it is. May I mention once more that most people nowadays use cars to run errands. They ride their horses only for pleasure."

Freddie laughed. John Henry loved to complain. "May I remind you that it is only two miles to town. Besides, I know Miss Mary gives you carrots every time you go in." Miss Mary was the PostMistress.

Freddie harnessed the horse to a small dogcart and Pirate jumped up on the seat. She tucked the telegram in the seat pocket. "Bring this to Miss Mary, please."

"All right," Pirate barked. "Hurry up, horse. We have a job to do."

John Henry moved out into a civilized walk, no faster. "There is nothing more boring than a dog who has a mission," he commented to no one in particular.

"Thank you," Freddie called to the departing twosome.

Chapter Two

Caroline comes to Boggy Creek.

Caroline Thompson was both pretty and popular. She did well in school and if she used her charm occasionally rather than hard work, she can be forgiven. She was kind to younger children, generous by nature and a very good person to have as a friend.

During the school year she lived in Washington, D.C. She'd been to the Capitol building and all the monuments many times. She danced in ballet class three afternoons a week. On the other days she played with her friends and rode her bike and did all the things that young ladies like to do.

She had a Mother and Father who loved her. A cozy brick house to live in and just about everything a little girl could want except a pet. Her Mother was even allergic to fish. Still, Caroline knew she was lucky.

During the summers she went to Camp Meadowlark where she stayed the entire month of July. Her parents always entered a balloon race during that time. Caroline liked to balloon sometimes. The world looked like a colorful patchwork quilt from so high up. But she preferred trail riding and swimming and performing in the Camp Talent Show.

This year her parents were in a TransAtlantic Race from New York to France. All the girls in her bunk gathered every night to watch the race on television. Her parent's purple and green balloon had been up in the front everyday.

That is how it happened that Caroline saw the terrifying storm that scattered the huge balloons like dried leaves on a windy day. And that was the last time anyone saw her parents.

A week later Caroline cried quietly on the southbound train.

She was being sent to her Aunt Freddie. The Head of the Camp had told Caroline that Aunt Freddie was her Guardian. Caroline had never met her Aunt and she was a little afraid. Caroline's Mother always said Freddie was crazy living as she did. They never visited her and Freddie never left her home in the woods. Her Father said she wasn't crazy, but Freddie was his sister so he'd have to say that. Caroline wondered if she acted like the old woman who lived on their street corner and mumbled to herself all the time.

So she worried about meeting her lunatic Aunt, and worried even more about her parents. She imagined them lost at sea, bobbing around in the balloon's basket, as hungry sharks circled waiting for the straw basket to sink.

But tears run out eventually and the train made a comforting click clack as it chugged down the tracks. The friendly Porter looked in on her often and the trip slowly turned into an adventure instead. She even looked forward to going to bed, in the bunk that folded up so tidily against the wall of her cabin in the day time.

As the train rushed on through the night, she dreamt her parents hiked through the jungle. Her Mother sneezed the entire time. In her dream, Father said they would be home as soon as they could. When the Porter woke her in the morning she felt a bit more cheerful. Even if it was only a dream, it was a comforting one.

There was only time for a quick breakfast as her stop was coming up. Her Aunt lived in a town named Boggy Creek. As the train pulled into the station, she saw the town was small and old fashioned, as if time had come to a standstill fifty years before.

The kind Porter helped Caroline with her suitcase and took her into the tiny station office. A bearded old man, the Stationmaster, was talking to an even older woman. She held a pretty little poodle in her arms.

The Stationmaster, Mr. Goodheart, smiled at Caroline. "Well, what can we do for you, young lady?"

Caroline thought his soft drawling accent delightful. The Porter looked worried.

"This little girl's Aunt is supposed to come fetch her and I've got to get back to the train."

"Well, the train got in early for once. Why don't you tell me who her Aunt is. I know most everybody round these parts."

"Fredricka Thompson." Caroline piped up.

The old lady clucked her tongue, "The witch woman, you mean."

Mr. Goodheart frowned, "Emmeline Harridan, now don't you go scaring the young lady. Freddie ain't no witch, and you were happy enough to use that poultice she gave you. As I recall you said your joints don't give you any misery now."

"That's true enough," Miss Emmeline replied, "but unnatural things happen around Fredricka Thompson."

The Stationmaster winked at Caroline. "It's true unusual things happen round Freddie but I don't know as that's a bad thing. Look, here she comes now." He pointed and they saw a strange procession coming down the street.

Caroline's and the Porter's mouths dropped open.

It was not the elegant horse pulling a beat up old cart that surprised them. Nor was it the handsome woman in a baseball cap who was deep in conversation with a black dog the size of a small bear! What amazed them was that the horse wore no bridle of any kind!

Not that it needed a bridle, Caroline thought. The horse pulled off the road exactly in front of the station.

"Unnatural, like I said." Miss Emmeline sniffed. "Well, I must be going. Good luck to you girl." With a heave, the older lady lifted her substantial bulk and walked down the steps as the wagon stopped in front of the station.

"How are the joints, Miss Emmeline? Hello, Mitzi." Aunt Freddie's voice was deep as a man's but friendly.

"Passable. You might hurry a bit. There's a young gal waiting for you in the office."

Freddie smiled widely and Caroline thought she looked beautiful. "Caroline is here! Good day to you, Miss Emmeline." Freddie took the steps two at a time and hurried into the office.

Her smile was warm and welcoming and she held out open arms to her niece. "Caroline! I'm your Aunt Freddie. I'm so glad you've come."

Caroline hugged her shyly and the Porter stepped forward.

"If you'll just show me your Driver's License, Ma'am, I'll leave her with you."

Freddie laughed. "You'll have to take my word for it. I don't have one. John Henry does all my driving."

The Porter looked perplexed. This situation was not covered in his manual. "Maybe I could see John Henry's license."

The Stationmaster snorted with laughter. "I'll vouch for her. This is the one and only Freddie Thompson who lives in these parts."

The train whistle blew impatiently and the Porter made his decision. "Just sign here, Ma'am."

Caroline noticed her Aunt's signature was full of grand leaps and loops.

The Porter touched the brim of his hat in farewell. "Glad to know you, Caroline. Hope you like living in the South."

"Thank you." Caroline said politely.

Freddie picked up Caroline's heavy suitcase easily. "We've got to be moving along now. I'm sorry, Mr. Goodheart, but we can't stay to chat. John Henry didn't want to come into town today. You know how difficult he can be."

Caroline wondered who John Henry was.

Mr. Goodheart scratched one bristly ear and winked at Caroline. "Now I'm counting on you to come visit me, Caroline. Maybe you'll get your Aunt to come into town more often."

"Once a week is plenty for me," Freddie replied. "Things are more peaceful at The Hollow." Caroline could hear the capital letters. "Come along now. We mustn't keep John Henry waiting." Caroline hustled to keep up with her Aunt's long legs as they walked to the wagon.

"Who is John Henry, Aunt Freddie?" She asked. "Is he your husband?"

Her Aunt looked startled for a moment, then started to laugh. Her horse wrinkled his nose showing long, yellow teeth, and the dog made a noise that sounded just like a chuckle. Freddie tossed the suitcase into the dogcart, then petted the horse's shining flank.

"Caroline, I want you to meet John Henry. John Henry, this is Caroline. She's come to live with us."

John Henry looked at Caroline and bobbed his head once. The dog barked sharply, looking cross.

"Oh, pardon me. I certainly didn't mean to forget you." Aunt Freddie sounded quite serious. Maybe she really was crazy, Caroline thought.

Her Aunt went on, "This is the King. He wants you to know that he doesn't care for being woken from his nap. But if you give him biscuits often, he'll be your friend and watch out for you."

Caroline decided since Aunt Freddie took this seriously so would she. Her Aunt might be bonkers but it was a nice bonkers. "How do you do, King. I promise I'll give you a biscuit as soon as I have one to give."

The dog smiled, showing a set of teeth that would have made Red Riding Hood's wolf jealous.

Aunt Freddie smiled. "You certainly know the right thing to say. You'll fit in at The Hollow just fine."

There was something special about that simple name, The Hollow. A warm glow filled Caroline when she heard it. She grinned at her Aunt. It seemed strange and magical things were the stuff of everyday to her Aunt Freddie.

They got in the wagon and John Henry looked back at them.

"It would be nice, John Henry, to get an ice cream on the way home. It is warm out." Freddie suggested.

It was as hot and damp as only August in the South can be.

The horse shook his head. His heavy mane flopped from side to side.

"I could pick up a few apples when we stop." Aunt Freddie coaxed.

At this the horse cocked his head and looked interested.

"Three and not one more or we'll do without ice cream." Her voice had a no-nonsense tone now.

John Henry started the wagon to Mr. Sweete's Soda Fountain down the street. His tail swished in a self-satisfied way, as though he had gotten the better part of the deal.

Caroline decided if her Aunt was crazy, then so were her animals. They thought they understood her!

Each of them had an ice cream, including the King. He ate his in two large bites. Aunt Freddie commented that he wouldn't be so heavy if he wasn't so greedy. The King ignored her and put his head in Caroline's lap. His tail wagged when she rubbed his ears in the ideal spot.

Three perfect red apples were placed in John Henry's feed bag. Freddie carefully inspected each one for bruises. "He won't touch them otherwise," she explained, "He's very fussy."

John Henry paraded grandly down the street. The PostMistress called hello to him and he whinnied back. The King barked at the woman and she blew him a kiss.

"John Henry usually comes with Pirate to pick up the mail. Pirate is the King's younger brother. They both are social butterflies and The Hollow is a bit quiet for them sometimes. Today however, the King announced he was coming, and Pirate had to guard the house. You should consider it an honor. The King doesn't go to town for just anyone."

Caroline was completely caught up in her Aunt's enchantment and threw her arms around the dog. "Oh, thank you for coming, King!"

For a moment, she could have sworn the dog said, "You're welcome." Caroline looked at her Aunt in confusion. "He said, *'You're welcome.'*"

"Of course, he did. Kings always have very fine manners. John Henry, if you are finished with your apples, could we go a bit faster? There are chores waiting back home for some of us."

The horse moved obligingly into a trot. He carried them down a shady lane, where tall oaks created a leafy canopy and Spanish Moss dripped mysteriously from the reaching branches.

They had gone only a couple of miles when suddenly the Myrtle bushes on the side of the road divided. John Henry turned onto a dirt driveway that Caroline was sure had not been there a second before. The bushes closed in behind them as they went past.

Caroline watched as the Myrtles moved back in place. She glanced up at her Aunt but did not say anything. Aunt Freddie certainly looked as if this was nothing out of the ordinary.

All the creatures of The Hollow turned out to meet her. She met shy Ace, with his long black hair that draped halfway to the ground, who thought himself delicate and frail, despite being the size of a small pony. Sable and Beautiful Maria, refined in appearance but tough as rawhide beneath their dark silken coats. Tess and Speed gaily licked her cheeks in welcome and the handsome red Pirate nudged her often for pats. Even John Henry wuffled her smooth hair in a friendly way.

Late that night Freddie tucked Caroline into her soft featherbed and kissed her goodnight.

"Aunt Freddie, do you think my parents are O.K.?" Caroline asked anxiously. She was sure if anyone would know Aunt Freddie did.

"I'm sure they are. We just need to keep believing so." Freddie prayed she was right. She kissed Caroline goodnight and left the room with the door ajar. New rooms are friendlier with the door left open a crack.

Caroline lay awake in the moonlight. She hugged the velvety cat who curled up beside her.

In the other room, a dog growled softly and she heard her Aunt say, "Yes, it's lovely having Caroline here."

Caroline fell asleep with a smile on her heart shaped face.

Chapter Three

A day on the River.

From the moment she arrived, to this very day, Caroline loved The Hollow. From the strange tree-shrouded driveway, to the darling, shingled cottage that was larger on the inside than the outside. An enormous oak tree grew right in the middle of the living room and straight out the roof. No matter how hot it was outside, inside was always wonderfully shady and cool.

Red Cardinals, iridescent Bluebirds, gentle, brown Mourning Doves and pale gray Mockingbirds that sang at night, nested in the broad branches overhead. Caroline often sat with Esmerelda and watched the doings at the birdbath, a most busy spot in the afternoons. The Cardinals always bathed one after another. The Bluebirds bathed together and one tiny brown Wren liked to splash and play until the birdbath needed to be refilled.

Esmerelda had endless patience for bird watching. The old cat made wickedly funny comments about the *flying pillows stuffed with fluff* that made Caroline laugh until her sides hurt. She loved the birds herself but they did act very silly sometimes. They were positive everyone wanted to eat them.

Caroline was not at The Hollow two days before every animal's voice became clear to her. When she asked her Aunt why that was, Freddie said it was just that she had never really listened before. You had to listen with your heart as well as your ears. So Caroline listened to all of them as hard as she could.

The King, Pirate and John Henry were her best friends. She loved all of the dogs but Ace spent most of his time alone in the back room, only coming out to visit with Aunt Freddie. The younger ones, Tess and Speed, were usually involved in a fast paced game of tag. Their Mother, Sable and her sister, Beautiful Maria had an ongoing feud with the local squirrels and rarely had time to chat except at night.

Caroline asked why they were allowed to terrorize the squirrels. It didn't seem quite fair, not in a place like The Hollow.

Freddie thought for a moment, then replied. "You have to accept folks for who and what they are. Everyone and everything has its shortcomings."

Caroline looked confused so her Aunt continued. "My shortcoming is I care for most people less than that pesky Cardinal who wants to nest inside the cottage. The King's bad point is he's grouchy and enjoys frightening the other dogs when he's in a bad mood. But he is the King and it is in his nature. Just as it is in Sable's and Maria's nature to hunt, though I don't believe in it myself."

"So you just love them for being themselves." Caroline said.

Freddie grinned. "Most of the time at any rate. Ask me again after they've dug up the entire garden."

Every morning it was Caroline's job to weed the large vegetable garden. Her Aunt Freddie was not at her best in the mornings and rarely spoke over her cup of coffee. Afterwards, Caroline fed John Henry his grain. He always gave her a gentle horse kiss with his whiskery nose.

A swim in the Waterhole, kept clear by a bubbling stream, was next. The King always kept her company though he wouldn't swim, he just sat in the water up to his neck. She only swam at the Waterhole. Her Aunt told her that snakes and alligators were not allowed there. Caroline learned early on it was pointless to ask why. That's just the way things were at The Hollow.

She explored the thick pine woods and along the rambling river with Pirate, and if it was cool enough, the King as well. Her Aunt said if she listened to the dogs she shouldn't get in any trouble.

One day they wandered far up Boggy Creek. As they started to cross a stream on a fallen tree, Caroline slipped and almost fell in. Pirate grabbed her shirt and tugged her back. Somehow she managed to regain her balance and back away.

Just ahead, in the warm, shallow water was a nest of poisonous Cottonmouth snakes. They swam and intertwined lazily, waiting for prey. The King said the snakes weren't really interested in little girls but they tended to bite when they were scared. Pirate said they were so stupid it did not take much to frighten them. Caroline shuddered at her close call. Cottonmouths were even more lethal than Rattlesnakes.

'No point in hunting trouble, you'll find it most times without even trying." The King advised sagely.

Caroline observed the nest from a safe distance. She tried to listen with her heart. She heard nothing. Caroline tried harder, squeezing her dark eyes shut, when she heard a faint hissing voice.

"I hope a frog swims by soon, I'm hungry."

"I hope it's a juicy fish," said another.

"Well, I'm going to catch a mouse if nothing swims by soon," said a third.

The snakes' thoughts were purely of dinner.

Pirate interrupted her concentration. "Let's go, there are better things to see than that nasty bunch of worms."

As they continued on their way a deep, rich voice called to Caroline. "Come swim little girl, the water is warm." The voice was hypnotic and Caroline's feet began to take her to the water's edge.

The King barked contemptuously and shattered the spell. "Go away, you overgrown lizard. Do you think we'd let Caroline fall for your old tricks?"

Pirate barked ferociously in agreement.

Caroline stopped when the King spoke.

"Don't listen to those garbage-eaters, little girl. The water is fine." The strange voice had a tinge of irritation in it and was no longer so inviting.

"I'm going to tell Freddie that you want to eat her kin, Lucifer. She'll make this river a mighty unpleasant spot for you." The King's hackles were raised and his tail was stiff.

"The little girl is family?" The voice asked.

"That's right. She's not for the likes of you. Go back down river. You're not welcome here." The King now stood protectively in front Caroline.

What Caroline thought was a floating log, suddenly blinked, and slithered into the slow current. Caroline realized it was an alligator, like she'd seen at the zoo, and at least twelve feet long!

"I like to eat dogs, too. Especially fat ones." Lucifer's huge mouth opened and shut with a loud snap. Caroline shivered a little. Lucifer seemed to have a thousand sharp teeth.

"You couldn't even catch a blind, crippled dog, Gator. Scare someone else. You sure don't scare us." The King acted unimpressed but he kept a sharp lookout until Lucifer swam out of sight.

"You don't think I'm fat, do you Caroline?" The King asked worriedly after the alligator was gone.

Caroline kissed his soft, furry cheek, grateful to have such a steadfast protector. "I think you're perfect."

The King smiled toothily at her.

The put-put sound of a motorboat sounded along the river and an old wooden fishing boat appeared. Written in fancy letters on the bow was the name Freddie.

Pirate ran back and forth on the bank, barking excitedly. Caroline noticed even The King looked unusually pleased.

"Captain Jeff! Captain Jeff! We're over here." Pirate called.

The boat headed towards them. The man at the big, wooden steering wheel was extremely tall, deeply tanned, with pale blond hair, stiff with saltwater, sticking out in every direction. His face was rough and weather-beaten but his smile was that of a boy Caroline's age.

"Ahoy, Pirate. Ahoy, King. Who's the new crew mate?" Captain Jeff idled the boat close by.

"This is Caroline, Captain. She lives with us now. We're showing her everything in Boggy Creek." Pirate told him.

"Pleased to meet you, Caroline."

Caroline, feeling shy, said how do you do. Captain Jeff was her Aunt's boyfriend. Freddie had his picture on the fireplace mantle.

The Captain's light blue eyes sparkled like sunlight on the sea. "I'm great friends with Freddie and I'm sure you and I are going to be great friends too. How did you come to stay at The Hollow?"

"Freddie is my Aunt. She's been taking care of me."

"Fantastic!" The Captain beamed. "I'd forgotten Freddie has a niece. Why don't you come aboard and I'll give you a ride home. I'm ready to set my feet on dry land for a while. Been out three weeks in the Gulf." He lowered a long plank to the shore and the two dogs bounded up it. Caroline walked up the wobbly board more carefully.

"I saw Lucifer swimming downstream. He hasn't been giving you any trouble has he?" The Captain asked. "I told that Gator last time if he bothers anyone at The Hollow I'd turn him into a pair of sea-boots. They'd be waterproof for sure." He laughed.

"He tried to get Caroline to go swimming but we sent him packing," said The King sternly.

"Now Caroline, most of the Gators round here are shy fellows and keep to themselves but Lucifer is different." The Captain looked at her shrewdly. "You heard that silky voice of his, didn't you?" Captain Jeff nodded at the surprise on her face. "You just stay close to The King and Pirate. They won't be duped by that sneaky relic."

Captain Jeff let Caroline steer the boat all the way back to the landing at The Hollow. He tooted the horn twice as they approached. Freddie and all the animals ran down the flower bordered path to greet them. The Captain expertly parked the boat while Freddie tied the mooring ropes securely to the narrow dock.

The Captain wasted no time. He jumped ashore and gave Freddie a big hug and kiss. Caroline decided the nicest kind of men were tall and loved the sea.

"So you didn't tell me you were having a visitor this summer." Captain Jeff said to Freddie. "Especially such a pretty one." He ruffled Caroline's hair.

"It was a surprise of the most delightful kind." Freddie put her arm around Caroline, who squeezed her back. Her Aunt always said nice things like that. It was part of her magic.

"I think she should stay forever," Pirate chipped in, as he nosed Captain Jeff for a pat.

All the dogs barked in agreement and John Henry whinnied loudly.

Caroline wished for a moment that she could stay there always, though she really did miss her parents and worried about them all the time. Everyday Caroline waited for Mailman Bob, hoping to hear from them. But she adored living at The Hollow with her eccentric relative.

Life was different at The Hollow. Aunt Freddie never cared if she made her bed and never asked if she'd washed her hair. Caroline always did but she didn't have to. There was no particular bed time at The Hollow either. But Caroline rarely stayed up late, after exploring and swimming all day she almost fell into her bed at night.

In the evenings she read. Freddie did not have a television. When her dark lashes began to flutter sleepily, Aunt Freddie would suggest that it was more comfortable to sleep on a bed than a couch. Esmerelda, who always slept with Caroline, cozier than any stuffed animal, would bat her nose gently until she got up and went to bed.

Tonight, with Captain Jeff here, Caroline knew they would stay up late. He brought enormous swordfish steaks for dinner. All the dogs watched hungrily as he grilled the fish. The cat wore an expression of utter bliss.

The steaks were greedily devoured under the giant oaks. The dogs all gulped theirs, then begged Captain Jeff and Caroline for more. Their begging was effective. The Captain and Caroline handed out tidbits. The dogs left Freddie strictly alone. She never gave out anything until she finished eating, so it was no use asking. Esmerelda ran with her portion into the house so the dogs wouldn't be tempted to steal it. Caroline ate a huge chunk, it was so delicious. Fish tasted wonderful fresh off the fire, much better than it did with sauces like she'd had back home.

They stuffed themselves full with fish, corn on the cob and crisp green beans. When they could eat no more, the Captain built up the fire with crackling pine logs. The flames' light danced along the huge tree trunks. Aunt Freddie brought out coffee for herself and the Captain, and cocoa for Caroline. Captain Jeff settled into a big chair. Pirate and The King curled up at his feet. Tess and Speed stopped their endless game of tag and joined the group. All the animals got comfortable and looked at him expectantly.

"Go on now, tell us your tale," ordered Sable, who was rather bossy on occasion. "You have a new one, don't you?"

"Please do, Jeff," Freddie asked. "Caroline has never heard one of your stories.

The Captain took Freddie's hand in his, and Esmerelda jumped on his lap.

"It just so happens that something extraordinary did occur this trip. You know how you hear the animals speak, clear as you and me, here at The Hollow?" He said to Caroline. "I'm not like Freddie. When I'm far out to sea the magic isn't as strong. Oh, I still can sense what they want but not in plain English."

"Well, one night as I slept on my bunk I heard a queer high pitched cry for help. I woke up thinking maybe it was a dream, but I heard it again. I turned on the big flood light and rushed up on deck. The moon was full, which helped, but I couldn't see anyone's head bobbing in the water. I yelled, '*Where are you?,*' loud as I could. 'Here. Here,' the voice squealed. I turned the boat and spotted a dolphin caught up in a nylon net."

"Now, some foreign countries use nets twenty miles long and strip the sea of everything. They just throw out what they don't want but not before it's dead. Even worse, they sometimes lose the net or sections of it. It's a terrible thing.

"Well, I jumped out of the boat, quick as a flash, and cut that poor Fin loose with my knife. Fins are what they call themselves, he told me. He did a couple of backflips, he was so happy to be free, than swam over and thanked me."

"How can you understand me? No man ever has before." The Fin was curious. I found out later his name was Wavedancer.

"I think my Lady's magic rubbed off on me," I told him. "She'd understand you, for sure."

"We need to get rid of this net, man," he said. "I have been caught in it all day. Without you I would have drowned."

"Dolphins, you see, need to breathe the same as you and me. Anyways, I'd been counting on picking up that net before it killed some other poor creature, and I told him so. We joined up as a team for the next few days. I gathered the net in the boat while he freed the snags that caught on the reef. We pulled in a few miles worth all told. Made me so furious, I could have keelhauled the fool who lost it." The Captain glowered and Caroline was glad it wasn't she he was angry at. Then his stormy expression cleared like the sky after a squall. "After we finished collecting the net, I thought old Wavedancer would clear out. But sure as the salt on my whiskers, he stayed with me the whole voyage. It's positively uncanny how that Fin knows where the shrimp and fish are. Made my best haul ever."

"Wavedancer sounds so cool. I wish I could meet him." Caroline said. "Can you imagine a dolphin taking you for a ride, Aunt Freddie?"

"I can." Freddie smiled. "It's too bad you didn't bring your friend, Jeff. The mullet are running and he'd enjoy the fishing."

Dolphins often ventured up the freshwater rivers on the coast in search of the tasty small fish.

"Then it's a good thing I invited him. He said he'd get here tomorrow. He wanted to tell his Mother he was all right first." The Captain looked very pleased with himself and leaned over to kiss Freddie's cheek. "Now whose turn is next?"

John Henry snorted in the darkness. "I want to tell Caroline how I met Freddie." The horse came forward and carefully lay down amongst the dogs.

"You know your Aunt used to be a horse trainer, rode in competitions and such." Caroline nodded, she'd seen photos of her Aunt jumping horses over enormous obstacles. John Henry was in many of them. "Well, I started my career at the racetrack."

"I thought this was about you meeting Freddie, not your whole life story, John Henry. We've all heard it before," Sable said.

"Over and over," Beautiful Maria added.

"Hush now, you two. Caroline hasn't heard it." Freddie patted the cushions next to her. "Come sit with me and we'll hear it again."

Sable was heard to mutter, "Conceited horse loves to talk about himself." But she and Maria curled up with their heads in Freddie's lap.

John Henry tossed his head arrogantly, "As I was saying, before those rodent chasers so rudely interrupted, I started out as a race horse. I could have been one of the greats!" His dark eyes gleamed proudly.

"And won the Kentucky Derby, no doubt." Sable snickered. A stern glance from Freddie quelled further remarks.

The horse ignored the dog. "The trainer, who took care of me, couldn't tell a lame horse from a sound one if it fell down in front of him. So he ran me one day when I had a sprain and that washed up my chances at the track. After I was well I was sold to a young girl who rode at the Horse Shows. They like beautiful horses at the Horse Shows. We won blue ribbons often." John Henry looked so smug, Caroline giggled.

"But the little girl grew up and went away and I was sold. Now I can't say the woman who bought me was cruel. She gave me pounds and pounds of carrots. Many more than I ever see around here." He gave Freddie a pointed look. "But the woman was terrified by riding! I still don't understand why she didn't just buy a pony and stick it out in her yard. That lady kept the reins so tight, my mouth was raw. I have a very sensitive mouth, you understand. She didn't even let loose over the jumps. Hit me hard with the bit every time." John Henry grimaced horribly to emphasize his point. "Before long I'd had enough of that, and I stopped jumping. So her trainer got on and hit me with a stick. I dropped him in the dirt a couple of times. After the third time he was so mad, he yelled, 'I'd sell you for a dollar, if I had a buyer.' Freddie was there. She walked up to me and asked, "What is your problem, horse?"

"So I told her, "They tear up my mouth something awful. I want a new home." Freddie gave the trainer a dollar, and took me straight home from there."

"I was afraid he'd change his mind if I didn't." Freddie added.

"I was the most successful horse she ever rode. Jumped in all the big cities, St. Louis, New York, Lexington, Los Angeles, you name it."

"Washington, D.C.?," Caroline asked. "That's where I come from."

"We placed first there, right Freddie?" John Henry queried.

"That's right, dear." Freddie affirmed.

"Why don't you compete any more?" Caroline wondered. She thought winning money and fancy ribbons sounded thrilling.

"John Henry and I aren't so young. Accidents happen and my bones don't heal so fast any more."

John Henry snorted with disbelief. "Don't you let her fool you, Caroline. She just got tired of dealing with people all day. She stills runs me like she was your age."

Freddie did not argue.

Caroline yawned. It was late. Esmerelda stretched and jumped off the Captain's lap.

"Caroline, it's time you took me to bed," the little cat announced. Caroline bent down to pick her up, and went inside.

After she brushed her hair and teeth, Caroline looked out the window. The Captain and her Aunt sat next to each other with the firelight on their faces. They looked very happy.

"Hurry up and switch off the lamp." Esmerelda complained sleepily.

So Caroline climbed in bed, pulled up the covers and did just that.

Chapter Four

A Voyage with the Captain.

The next morning Wavedancer arrived as promised. He wore a huge grin and squeed with excitement when Captain Jeff suggested they spend the day on the boat. Caroline and Freddie were as enthusiastic as the Fin.

The King and Pirate jumped aboard right away. They often voyaged with the Captain. The other dogs choose to stay behind. Maria said she and Sable were busy. A ground squirrel family wanted to move into the oak at the cottage. That was completely unacceptable. The two of them trotted purposefully off into the woods. Ace did not leave his room

"It's so boring sitting still on the boat all day," said Tess.

"Stay and play with us, Caroline." Speed put in.

Caroline said thank you but she wanted to go. The two young dogs began a game of 'Keep Away' with an old dishrag.

Captain Jeff busied himself in the kitchen, making lunch. Freddie and Caroline made sure those who stayed behind had enough food and water. The two of them giggled when they saw the enormous pile of sandwiches the Captain made. It looked like enough for a dozen people. Freddie baited him, asking if they were going away for a whole week, not just the day.

"We wouldn't be eating at all if I left it up to you," he teased back. Freddie hated to cook. Dinner was always something easily put together. Caroline didn't mind though. The cookie jar was always kept full.

Soon they were ready with a full picnic basket, towels, sodas and plenty of sunblock. The Captain cast off, and with Wavedancer leading the way they headed down river.

In a few miles the water became very clear and cold for late summer. The Captain explained the temperature stayed 75 degrees because of the underground springs. Caroline and Freddie jumped into the river. Cold-blooded snakes and alligators hated chilly water, so it was safe to swim.

Caroline paddled slowly around the boat when she suddenly felt herself lifted right out the water! Wavedancer had swum up beneath her.

"Hang onto my fin." He squeed and she gripped tightly. He took her faster and faster, surfing the water's surface. She shrieked with delight as the water sprayed around them. He gave Freddie a ride, too. She shouted as loudly as Caroline had. The Fin was enchanted by Freddie's long hair and wrapped the tendrils around his snout.

Captain Jeff shook his finger at the dolphin and ordered him to stop flirting. That set them all off into a fresh burst of giggles.

Wavedancer told them he had some friends who wanted to see them. "Just a little farther," he said.

The Fin chased and leaped after schools of mullet as they traveled along the shoreline. He looked adorable with fish sticking out of each side of his mouth like cigars. Finally he swam up to the boat.

"Anchor here, Captain. I'll fetch my friends." He dove beneath the surface and disappeared.

"Who are his friends?," asked Caroline.

"Most likely the other members of his pod," Freddie guessed. Pods are the family groups dolphins live with.

Captain Jeff grinned. "You'll both just have to wait and see." The Captain already knew about the surprise.

In a few minutes the Fin returned. "These are my friends, Gentle and her son, Floater." Two serious whiskered faces emerged from the river beside him. Caroline realized they were Manatees. Sometimes they were called seacows because they ate the grass on the river bottom. Freddie swam up to Gentle and put one hand on the large mammal's neck. Gentle weighed over a thousand pounds. The wise old Manatee smiled. "I haven't seen you in a long time, Freddie."

"You didn't come to visit this year. I've been hoping you were all right." Every year many Manatees were killed by careless boaters. To stay warm the Manatees had to sun themselves at the surface. That made it easy for them to be run over. Every year there were fewer and fewer of the kindly creatures. And every year there were more boats.

"Me and mine have been keeping well, praise all." Gentle told her. "But we decided not to go North this summer. Too many power boats. My oldest boy was hurt badly by a propeller, but he's better now."

Caroline noticed both of the manatees had long white scars from propellers on their backs. Floater came up out of the water right in front of her and looked at her with dark, liquid eyes. "Come play with me, little girl."

She dove in and Freddie tossed her a diving mask and snorkel. She put them on, then slid her arms around Floater's neck. He swam slowly just beneath the surface so Caroline could breathe. If a ride on Wavedancer was breathtaking, gliding with Floater was beautifully serene.

The seagrass waved slowly in the current and tickled her legs as they swam through. The water turned a brilliant turquoise blue at the mouth of the springs.

Crawdads, that looked like tiny lobsters, scurried busily about the riverbed.

Dark feathered Cormorants dove underwater to catch fish. Captain Jeff had told her in China they tamed the birds to catch fish for them. A ring was put around the bird's neck to keep it from swallowing the bigger fish. These wild birds had no such problem and ate fish much larger than looked possible with their thin necks. Several of the seabirds were up on the shore. They stood with their wings outstretched to dry their water-logged feathers.

A couple of grinning Pelicans scooped up their dinner beside them.

When Caroline's teeth chattered with cold, Floater returned to the boat. Freddie tossed a few heads of lettuce to the Manatees who graciously thanked her. Freddie commented that Manatees were the most polite creatures. Pirate and The King, who gobbled sandwiches as fast as the Captain handed them out, did not argue nor did they say thank you.

There were just enough sandwiches left for Caroline and Freddie to have two each. The King and Pirate lay in the cool shallows while the humans finished their late lunch. When the last wrapper was stowed and everything was shipshape, the Captain said it was time to head back. Gentle and Floater said good-bye and Caroline kissed each wet cheek. She hoped she would see them again.

Wavedancer walked on his tail, showing off. He was a little jealous of all the attention Gentle and Floater received, so Caroline kissed him too.

The week flew by with the Captain there. Every day they picnicked, and when the afternoon thunderstorms came they all sat in the cottage and ate popcorn while the Captain told them seafaring tales. Caroline felt badly that John Henry couldn't fit in the cottage and stayed in his barn alone during the rains. But the horse said he didn't mind. He preferred to nap in the afternoons.

Finally the sea's call grew too strong to resist. It was time for the Captain to leave. Wavedancer met him at the dock one morning. The Fin had acquired a taste for human company. The Captain hugged Caroline and Freddie then boarded his boat.

"Come back soon, Jeff." Freddie called. "Have a safe voyage."

The Captain touched his peaked hat with a jaunty grin, then turned the boat towards his beloved ocean.

"Aren't you lonely when he's gone?" Caroline asked.

"Sometimes. But you have to go where your heart leads you. The Captain would be like a caged Eagle if he stayed ashore, and just as ill-tempered. Besides, I never get any work done while he's here and it seems I'm wiping up muddy footprints the whole time." Freddie finished with a smile. Caroline grinned back. The Captain never wiped his feet before coming into Freddie's tidy cottage.

"Is that his shortcoming?" Caroline asked sassily.

"Among others, you smart thing. But I surely do miss the lovely breakfasts he cooks up."

Caroline nodded with a sigh. The Captain made delicious eggs and pancakes. It would be cold cereal until he came back again.

It was time to do all the things they had put off while the Captain was in port. The cottage needed a thorough cleaning. Caroline swept, while Freddie mopped the bleached wood floors. When everything sparkled and shined, Freddie sat down and fanned herself.

"Thank God, that's out of the way for another week. Caroline, be a dear, and get us some ice water, will you?"

They drank the icy spring water with pleasure as the dogs filed into the house that had been off limits during the house clean. They were discussing what to do next when a faint yapping sounded in the distance. The call grew louder and there was a harsh scratch on the front door.

"Freddie, Freddie, come quick!" They heard.

Caroline opened the door and Mitzi ran in. The poodle raced over to Freddie, panting heavily.

"Freddie, there's something wrong with Miss Emmeline! She fell down and won't get up!"

Freddie got up immediately. "I'm on my way. Come with me, Caroline. I might need you."

Caroline wrapped her arms tightly around her Aunt's waist as John Henry flew like the wind down the back lanes to Miss Emmeline's house. Caroline could well believe he might have been a famous race horse. Mitzi's ears blew back as she perched on Freddie's lap and Pirate raced alongside, keeping up easily. As fast as a horse can be, a Wolfhound is faster.

Freddie vaulted down from John Henry when they arrived at Miss Emmeline's immaculate white farm house. She pushed open the front door. In Boggy Creek they don't need to lock their doors.

Miss Emmeline lay on the kitchen floor. Her skin was gray but she was breathing, if barely.

Freddie felt helpless. She knew a fair amount about doctoring animals but something like this was quite beyond her.

Caroline hovered in the doorway. It was a little frightening how the old woman lay in an untidy heap on the floor.

"Caroline, Miss Emmeline doesn't have a phone so I need you to ride to the hospital in Hillsdale as quick as you can. Pirate knows the way." Freddie warned her, "The Magic grows weaker the further you get from The Hollow. You'll have to really ride. Can you do that? I need to stay with Miss Emmeline."

Caroline nodded, her mouth suddenly dry. John Henry was awfully big and if he didn't understand what she said, how could she make him do anything? But Aunt Freddie needed her.

"I'll help her." Pirate barked. The Magic touched dogs more strongly than horses. Probably because dogs have always been man's best friend. But Hillsdale was five miles from Miss Emmeline's and ten from The Hollow. There would be no Magic that far away.

"Hurry, Caroline. She needs real medical help. I know I can count on you."

Caroline raced outside behind Pirate. The dog told John Henry they had to get to the hospital as fast as they could. Caroline climbed up on the fence then jumped on John Henry's back. He took off as if he was in the starting gate on the race track. John Henry ran flat out down the narrow dirt road. Caroline's eyes watered from the wind and she twisted his mane securely between her fingers.

Freddie sat down on the floor next to Miss Emmeline and took the old lady's hand. It was all she could do. Mitzi licked her owner's wrinkled cheek.

Miss Emmeline stirred slightly. Her eyes opened and she looked confused. "Freddie, how did you come here?" Her voice was a dim whisper.

"Shh, Miss Emmeline. You fainted. Mitzi came and fetched me. Caroline is going for an Ambulance. You just rest now."

Miss Emmeline did not say anything but she squeezed Freddie's hand gratefully then shut her eyes.

Caroline held on as they galloped down the dirt road. She spoke to John Henry every few minutes and the horse answered her back, if briefly. He was breathing hard, his nostrils flared. Suddenly Pirate leaped off the road onto a path through the woods. "This ways shorter," he barked.

They jumped a huge fallen tree that blocked their path. Caroline felt herself slip but somehow she found John Henry's back when they landed. They rounded a curve at break neck speed.

"John Henry, slow down. I'm going to fall off." Caroline yelled.

The horse said nothing, nor did he check his speed. Caroline concluded nervously that they were beyond The Hollow's magic.

The dog raced on. They crossed narrow streams and wove through the trees. Branches scraped her bare legs. She had a deep scratch on her left thigh but she did not feel any pain. There was no time too. Suddenly, a large Fox squirrel with a black head and long silver tail ran in front of John Henry. The horse spooked violently sideways and Caroline tumbled off onto a thin carpet of dried leaves. The wind was knocked out of her. She gasped as she tried to catch her breath. John Henry stopped a little ways on looking at her in a confused manner, as if asking why she was on the ground. Pirate ran back.

He barked at her. Caroline did not understand what he wanted. Pirate yanked on her sleeve and she realized he wanted her to get up. She stood up, a little sore, but she was all right. A flash of Miss Emmeline stretched out on the hard floor gave her strength. She ran to John Henry but the horse shied at her approach and moved out of reach. Without magic John Henry was no more than an ordinary horse and not a very brave one at that!

At Camp Meadowlark, Caroline rode regular horses and to catch them she always gave them a treat. She didn't have anything with her but perhaps a handful of grass would do the trick. She tore off a big handful. John Henry's pricked forward and he stepped towards her. Once he was eating, Caroline looked at his tall back. How was she going to get back up? She had no rope to lead him and he wore no tack of any kind. She tugged on his forelock to make him walk over to a stump so she could mount. He set his feet stubbornly. For a moment Caroline wanted to cry but Aunt Freddie was counting on her. She pulled more grass and bite by bite, step by step, John Henry walked over to the stump. Pirate paced anxiously. Unlike the horse, the dog remembered his mission. Finally Caroline had John Henry next to the stump. She climbed up on it. The horse shifted uneasily swinging away from the stump.

"Whoa, John Henry, please." She pleaded, in the low soothing voice her Riding Instructor always used. Thankfully, it worked. She managed to clamber on his back.

Pirate barked sharply and took off. John Henry didn't move. Caroline kicked him hard with her bare heels and he broke into a canter following the dog. The horse stopped up abruptly at the next stream edge. Caroline slid far forward onto his neck but somehow managed to stay on. She pushed herself back behind his withers, then pounded him with her heels until he crossed the knee deep water. They were off and running again. They reached the main road shortly and Pirate headed straight to the Hospital. Caroline never noticed the surprised looks of the Hospital Personnel as she jumped off the horse. She was covered with sand and leaves.

"Pirate, keep John Henry from leaving." She called as she ran into the building.

The dog barked and Caroline felt hopeful that Pirate understood her even if she couldn't understand him.

She hurried to the front desk where a middle aged woman was sorting papers with a bored expression. "Please, we need an Ambulance, quick. I think she's dying. Oh, please hurry." Caroline gasped out.

The Receptionist was suddenly all business. "Where and who is she?"

"Miss Emmeline Harridan in Boggy Creek. We found her on the floor. She looks so bad." Now that she had made it to the Hospital the tears she had wanted to shed in the woods came involuntarily.

The Receptionist picked up the phone. "Get over to Emmeline Harridan's in Boggy Creek right away," she said into the receiver. "Possible heart attack." She hung up. "Don't worry young lady, they're on their way."

It seemed ages before the Ambulance came as Freddie waited anxiously. Finally, she heard the siren coming up the drive. Caroline, Pirate and John Henry galloped in moments later. The route through the woods was much more direct. As is usually the case, since Caroline was no longer in a hurry, the ride was completely uneventful.

The Paramedics bustled into the house in a professional manner and loaded the sick woman into the Ambulance. Freddie hugged Caroline, relieved to see her niece was all right despite looking as if she'd had a bad fall. "Thank you, dear. You were splendid."

Freddie gently squeezed Miss Emmeline's shoulder before the door closed. "I'll take good care of Mitzi till you're well." She assured her.

They rode home at a much more sedate pace. Poor John Henry dripped sweaty white lather. He apologized to Caroline repeatedly for dumping her on the ground. He said he grew so confused when he got too far from The Hollow. Caroline pet him and told him it was O.K.

"Well, at least we were in time. I was afraid she wouldn't make it." Freddie said. "I hope nothing is really wrong with Miss Emmeline."

"How come you are so nice to that mean old lady?" Caroline asked. "She calls you a witch."

"Oh, Miss Emmeline is just cranky because she's in pain. Her joints keep her in bed too many mornings. But she doesn't like anyone to pity her. It's not an easy thing growing old."

A few days later Pirate and Mitzi came down the driveway with Miss Emmeline herself. She had a tall chocolate cake in her hands.

Freddie hurried to meet her.

The old woman gave Freddie the cake. "I made this big enough for you and the girl and all your other creatures. Turns out I have high blood pressure. They just pricked and poked me like a pincushion, then sent me home with a bottle of pills. Mitzi looks real well. You do know a thing or two about caring for animals."

"Well, I must be going. Thursday is wash day. You and Caroline come visit me real soon. I'll make us strawberry shortcake. The berries are extra good this year." And with a quick pat for Pirate, Miss Emmeline and Mitzi departed.

Caroline looked after the old woman. "Jeez Aunt Freddie, she never even said thank you for all you did."

"Sure she did." Freddie lifted the cake with a smile. "Who wants a slice?"

Chapter Five

The Big Thunderstorm and what it brought.

The weather grew hotter and hotter. The cooling afternoon rains hadn't come for a week and the red line in the thermometer kept climbing. Even the cottage was warm. There was no air conditioning to cool it off. Air conditioners ruined the environment, Aunt Freddie said. If you were hot you jumped into the Waterhole. The dogs were in and out of the water all day like the pair of otters who lived up stream.

Caroline woke one morning feeling cross. It was already hot and sticky and the sun had not even cleared the tree tops. Not a puff of wind disturbed the shivering pine needles. Caroline wished she was back in her brick house in Washington where Mother kept the temperature no higher than 72 degrees.

She wandered into the kitchen with a sour face. Aunt Freddie had all ready finished her morning coffee and was setting up her easel for a day's work. She made her living painting pictures of the local wildlife and fauna. She put down her brush when she saw her niece.

"Why the long face?" Freddie asked.

Esmerelda threaded herself around Caroline's legs. "She's hot, Freddie." The cat explained. "She's not used to it like we are."

Caroline stroked the clever kitty. "Is it ever going to rain again?" She tried not to whine but was only partly successful.

"Why don't you go for a swim?" Her Aunt suggested.

"I don't feel like it," she pouted, feeling quite sorry for herself.

"It's going to rain," said the cat. "Lots and lots of rain. More than we've seen all summer."

Freddie turned to Esmerelda. "Is it going to be a big storm?"

The cat nodded and went back into the bedroom for her mid-morning nap that always followed her morning nap.

"I have a feeling, Caroline, we're going to have more rain than even you want. If Esmerelda says a storm is coming I guess we'd better get prepared. Now I want you to take a swim. Crabby children are even worse than crabby dogs. Go on now, chop chop."

The cool water did make her feel better and Caroline giggled when Speed and Tess ran by, splashing everyone. The King tried to nip them as they went past. He hated bad manners. But they dodged his gnashing teeth easily.

Suddenly the air chilled and thick black clouds gathered overhead.

"Everyone back to the cottage. Tess and Speed, that means you as well." Pirate said sternly to his daughters.

The first fat drops of rain began to fall and the sky let out a mighty blast of thunder. Caroline felt her arm hairs crackle. The dogs all bolted to the house and she sped after them.

Freddie was at the door. "Hurry everyone." The dogs poured past her into the shelter of the cottage. Caroline was not far behind. Already it was dark as night outside. Flashes of lightning outlined the tall pines in a spooky fashion.

The windows were hurriedly latched against the slashing rain, and small twigs and leaves blew past helter-skelter. A large branch fell on the front path with a loud crash and Caroline jumped a little, startled.

"It's going to be a big one." The King said worriedly and moved closer to Freddie on the sofa. He didn't like anyone to know but thunder scared him terribly.

The wind picked up, faster and wilder, till the world outside looked like a shaken snow globe. More branches fell, one on the roof. But the cottage was stoutly made and they were safe inside as long as they stayed away from the windows.

"Will John Henry be O.K.?" Caroline asked, concerned.

"He'll be fine." Freddie assured her. "He was inside his barn with the door shut long before you lot came in."

Thunder suddenly boomed so loudly, it sounded as if a bomb exploded in the front yard. Caroline clapped her hands over her ears. Even Freddie looked disquieted.

"I'll bet we've lost another Slash Pine. I hope none of the squirrels were hurt."

Sable and Maria nosed each other, smiling.

Lightning kept illuminating the sky but that was the only close hit. After an hour the wind died down and the rain turned into a steady downpour that watered the flowers and lawn.

"I hope we don't have too much damage. A half dozen trees were struck last year. The Cardinals lost their entire nest of eggs." Freddie fretted.

The rain let up into its regular friendly shower. The storm had passed.

"Can I go out now, please?," begged Tess.

"Open the door, Freddie." Sable demanded.

"O.K. O.K. But you're not coming back in soaking wet. The cottage doesn't need to stink of wet dogs." Freddie warned, then opened the door. The dogs raced out, almost knocking her over.

The rain finally stopped. The sun broke out in a blue, blue sky. The world looked and smelled freshly washed.

"May I see if John Henry is all right?," asked Caroline.

"Go ahead, dear. I'm going to check on the trees out back. You come get me if there's a problem." Freddie went out.the back door as Caroline headed to the barn.

She heard a loud whinny and began to run. "What's the matter, John Henry?," she called.

John Henry's head stuck out the barn door. "Caroline, come quick. There's an intruder in my house." He disappeared back into his stable and she could hear his hooves bang on the wall. She wondered if she should get her Aunt right away, then decided to check out the intruder first. The horse considered even the barn mice intruders.

She peered into the dark building. Under John Henry's kicking legs cowered a boy a little older than herself. He had curly, light brown hair and looked extremely frightened.

"John Henry, stop!" Caroline shouted. "You're scaring him."

The horse quit kicking but faced the boy in a threatening manner with his ears pinned flat back. "He trespassed, Caroline. Came in without so much as a by your leave. Sat on my alfalfa." The horse sounded highly aggrieved but he moved over for Caroline to enter.

The boy scrunched tight into the corner trying to stay away from the flying hooves. Even when John Henry backed up he made no move to leave.

"You better come with me. John Henry hates anyone touching his hay, you know." Caroline said in a friendly tone. The boy sat frozen, his eyes glued to the horse.

Caroline shook her head with impatience. "For Gosh sakes, do you want him to kick you? Come on." She went over to the boy and took his hand, dragging him out of John Henry's stable.

"He's ruined my hay, Caroline," the horse complained, nosing among the flattened alfalfa.

"Stay here," she told the boy. She quickly tossed a fresh flake to John Henry who muttered thank you around a big mouthful.

The boy tried to look tough. "Aren't you scared of that vicious horse? I'd have shot him if I had a gun."

Caroline looked at him stunned, then angry. "How dare you! Here you trespass in his house, sit on his food and then, when he didn't even hurt you, you want to shoot him. You are a dreadful boy. I'm going to tell Aunt Freddie to send you packing." Caroline had picked up The King's favorite expression. She turned to go.

"Wait. Wait a minute. I'm sorry I said I wanted to shoot your horse. I only went in the barn to get out of the rain. I sat on the hay cause it looked soft and all of a sudden he went crazy! Honest!" The boy begged.

"Well, you did ruin his dinner and he didn't try to hurt you. If he'd wanted to we wouldn't be here talking now. Don't you know horses take their dinner very seriously?" Caroline's voice sounded a little superior.

"I don't know anything about horses. I come from the City." The boy wiped the tears from his face, embarrassed. After all, Caroline was younger than him and a girl.

"What's your name?," she asked, "And what are you doing at The Hollow? No one comes here without an invitation."

The boy looked smug for a moment. "My name's Trent and I bet you have salesmen come here without an invite."

Caroline shook her head. "Never. Not here at The Hollow."

The King barked, startling them. "What's that boy doing here and why'd he ruin John Henry's dinner?"

"I don't know why he's here and he didn't mean to spoil the hay. He comes from the City." She explained.

"We'd better tell Freddie," said The King.

"That's what I was going to do." Caroline agreed.

"I'll go get her." The King trotted off.

The boy, Trent, looked at her as if she was crazy. Suddenly she knew how her Aunt felt sometimes.

"Who in tarnation are you talking to? And was that a dog? He was huge."

Caroline decided not to answer the first question. "The King is most certainly a dog. He's a Russian Wolfhound. They are very rare. Come on. You need to meet my Aunt Freddie."

Trent looked anxious. "Does she have to know? I can just leave."

Caroline giggled. "She already knows you're here. Why do you want to leave so fast? It's almost lunch time. Aren't you hungry?"

Freddie came around the corner just then. She surveyed the boy with a solemn expression. "Hello, Trent. The King says John Henry gave you quite a fright."

Trent stared at the tall woman stunned. He hadn't told her his name. "I wasn't scared much," he muttered, since of course he had been.

"Well, we were lucky, Caroline. None of our trees were hit. Why don't you both come to the house. We'll have some lunch and decide what to do with Master Trent, here."

She started off, obviously expecting the children to follow her. Caroline could hear Freddie mumble to herself.

"My, what a curious summer. Children arriving from God knows where. I wonder how he got into The Hollow. He must be touched with the Magic or the Myrtle bushes would never have let him in, storm or no storm."

Trent looked as if he wanted to run away.

"Come on," Caroline urged, "Aunt Freddie gets impatient if you don't do what she asks."

"She real strict?" Her words had not reassured him. Just the opposite in fact.

Caroline laughed in his face. "No, she isn't strict at all. But when she does ask she likes everyone to hop to. And we do."

"There other kids here?" Trent asked.

"No. I mean her animals." When she saw he wasn't coming, she grabbed his arm and pulled him along.

Trent's eyes darted around the peculiar cottage. It looked like something out of the Fairy Tales that his Mother read to him before she died. He wondered if the copper haired woman was a witch. Though he'd never heard of a witch who wore a baseball cap and cutoff shorts.

Freddie set out a loaf of bread, a wedge of cheese, and jars of peanut butter and jelly. "Help yourselves."

The children made sandwiches. Freddie cut a slice of cheese that she shared with The King. She let Trent finish his first sandwich before asking him any questions. The boy ate as if he was starving.

"Now Trent, why don't you tell us how come you're wandering around the woods alone. Your parents must be worried sick about you."

The boy looked sullen. "My Mother died a long time ago and my Father wouldn't worry. I'll bet he hasn't even noticed I'm gone."

"I see," Freddie pursed her lips, "Where are you from?"

"The City. And I'm not going back. You can't make me!" He cried.

Freddie looked mildly surprised. "I don't make anyone do anything. So what are your plans? Or are you just traveling?"

"I'd like a job but no one wants a thirteen year old working for them." He tried to sound brave but his voice cracked.

"I think we have some work that needs doing. I'll make you a deal. You tell me your whole name and phone number so I can call your Father and tell him you're O.K., and you may stay here and work in exchange for room and board."

Trent got up. "If I tell you, I'll have to go back, so I'm leaving." He stood and put the rest of his sandwich in his pocket. He'd had quite a few hungry days recently.

"Sit down, please." Freddie's tone was quiet but Trent found he was back in his seat before he could argue.

"Did I not just say that you could stay? Please listen more carefully. Now, your Father's name and number please."

The name and number seemed to volunteer themselves.

Freddie left the table. "I'm riding John Henry to town. Caroline will help you get settled. Put him in the spare room, sweet. Trent, I'm counting on you to stay until I get back. Do I have your word?"

Trent felt a little in awe of this matter-of-fact lady. "Yes, Ma'am."

"Very good. Then I'm off. Have another sandwich if you like," she said as she left.

They heard her yell, "John Henry!," and then the sound of galloping hooves.

"I'm not going back," Trent said again. "I'm clearing out soon as your Aunt gets home." He'd have to wait until then. He had given his word.

"Why?" Caroline asked. "It's so cool living here at The Hollow."

He looked at her in a superior way. "She just said I could stay. My Father will make me come back even if he doesn't miss me."

"If Aunt Freddie says you're staying, you are," she insisted stubbornly.

"No one can get my Father to do anything he doesn't want."

Caroline smiled smugly. "You don't know Aunt Freddie. Do you want some cookies and milk?"

They were still eating when Freddie got back. She sat down with them and took a chocolate chip for herself.

"Well, your Father was relieved to hear you were all right. 'Completely frantic', I believe were his very words."

"I won't be here when he comes." Trent's jaw stuck out, reminding Caroline of a bulldog.

Freddie looked confused. "Who said he was coming? I told him I thought you should stay here for a while."

"And he said yes? I don't believe you."

Freddie looked more severe than Caroline had ever seen her. "Young man, are you calling me a liar?"

"No, Ma'am." He replied, chastened.

Freddie's smile was always quicker than her frown. "Good. Now, you might as well start with your chores. You can paint the back door. Bright blue should look nice." All the doors were different cheerful colors. "Caroline, would you see to John Henry? He needs a bath and I didn't want to take the time arguing with him."

"Yes, Aunt Freddie." Caroline grinned as she went back to the barn. Trent didn't know anything about magic. The next few days were going to be such fun.

Pirate, The King and John Henry were gossiping about the newcomer.

"Very bad manners, him sitting on your dinner like that," said The King. "I'd've nipped him but good."

"He's just a puppy, doesn't know any better." Pirate reasoned.

"Aunt Freddie says he's going to stay with us for a while." Caroline told them.

"He'd better keep away from my alfalfa." John Henry snorted.

"I think he learned that lesson." Caroline giggled. "Now come let me wash you. You look so handsome when your socks are white and shiny." She had discovered that flattery was the best way to deal with the vain horse.

"That's very true." John Henry graciously allowed her to begin his bath.

Chapter Six

Trent meets Lucifer.

Trent was a very difficult boy, Caroline thought, in the first days that he was there. He had ignored all her friendly overtures and doggedly worked at every task Freddie gave him. Aunt Freddie said to give him time. That he was like Miss Emmeline, hurt and cranky, but he'd come around just like she did if they were patient. So Caroline tried to be, even if Trent barely replied to her most civil questions.

The first day or two Trent kept looking nervously over his shoulder, expecting his Father or more likely his Father's Assistant to come fetch him. After three days, though he wouldn't admit it even to himself, he was put out that his military like parent hadn't come.

This place was very weird, he thought. He stole a glance over at The King, who watched the two children weed the garden. Caroline and Miss Freddie talked to the animals as if they were people. And their pets. . . It was almost creepy, how they seemed to know what he was saying. He'd have been scared if they weren't so friendly. Even John Henry seemed to have forgiven him for sitting on the hay.

Freddie had Trent grain the horse for a day or so. A surefire method for gaining the horse's affections.

Caroline finished her section first. She sat on the ground and wiggled her toes in the damp, sandy soil.

"Hey Trent," she asked, "Why'd you run away?" Caroline had wanted to ask since he'd come but was leery of the older boy's temper. "Did your Father hit you or something?"

"No, he'd never do anything like that." Trent answered angrily, sticking up for his absent parent.

"Don't get mad. I just wanted to know why you left."

Trent stopped weeding and plopped down beside her.

"My Father is an important Businessman. He travels around the country, even to Europe, all the time. He's so busy, he never came once to see me play on the baseball team. He doesn't love me or anything. Our housekeeper, Mrs. Grumpe, takes care of me. At least she makes sure I have dinner and clean clothes. The rest of the time she shoos me out of all the rooms saying I shouldn't get her clean house dirty."

"He never saw you play? That's awful," Caroline sympathized. When she had danced in the ballet, The Nutcracker, last Christmas, her parents had come to almost every show. She suddenly missed them so much, tears welled up in her eyes and rolled down her cheeks.

"He never does anything with me. I'm just in his way." Now Trent's lips quivered.

"Will you two talk about something else for pity's sake." The King barked. "You're worse than a pair of weanling puppies."

"I am not crying," Caroline argued. The King looked at her with disbelief.

"God, I hate it when you do that." Trent muttered.

"Do what?"

"Act like that dog is talking to you."

Caroline pulled herself up proudly. "If you'd try to listen with your heart instead of your stupid ears you might just hear them yourself. Haven't you figured out that The Hollow is a special place? I'm going for a swim at the Waterhole. You still have some weeds left." Caroline walked off stiffly. Idiotic, know-it-all boy, she thought.

Trent was sorry he'd aggravated the younger girl. Miss Freddie and Caroline had been so nice since he'd come, never prying or nosy. He decided he'd apologize when he was done weeding and said so aloud.

"That's a smart idea, youngster. There might be hope for you yet." The King growled.

Trent shook his head. That dog couldn't have talked.

"You're just a dog. Dogs don't speak," he said.

The King got up and curled his lip at Trent with exasperation. "Foolish puppy." He stalked off with great dignity.

Trent suddenly felt very lonely and hurried to finish so he could join Caroline.

She accepted his apology quickly. She was sorry that she had gotten mad at him. After all he didn't have an Aunt to love him when his parents were gone like she did.

They spit on their hands and shook them.

"Pax," they both said.

"Do you want to explore along Boggy Creek? There are some really neat things to look at." She suggested, offering the branch of friendship.

"Yeah. Won't your Aunt mind?"

"Not if we go with Pirate and The King."

Permission was given in an absentminded way. Freddie was painting a portrait of Wavedancer.

The two dogs and children set off down the river path. Caroline felt very cool when she warned Trent about the Cottonmouth snakes who lived at the small pool.

He didn't believe her and was going to move closer when Pirate growled at him. "Boy, I've been taking your side but you do some crazy things. One bite from that snake and you'd be spending the night at the hospital. That's a terrible place, smells awful."

Trent looked at the red dog with amazement, "You can talk!"

"We all can. What did you think?" Pirate asked surprised.

"He thought we were dumb animals." The King put in dryly.

Caroline just smiled broadly.

The day was warming up and Caroline felt a trickle of sweat slide down her back. "Let's go home for a swim."

"There's plenty of water here," Trent objected, "Just go in the river."

"Aunt Freddie told me not to. There are dangerous things in the river."

"I bet you do everything your Aunt tells you, like a goody-goody. There's nothing in the water. I'll show you." Before Caroline or the dogs could stop him, Trent jumped right in.

He paddled out deeper and treaded water. "Come on in. The water's great."

Caroline saw a floating log start towards the boy. The King spotted Lucifer at the same time. "Trent look out, there's an alligator!" She cried.

"Boy, start swimming fast!" The King ordered and stepped into the shallows, ready to fight.

Trent looked over his shoulder and saw Lucifer approaching swifter than he would have believed possible. Terrified, he swam as fast as he could. He choked on a mouthful of water but didn't slow down. The skin on his back crawled hideously. He could feel the alligator close on him.

Caroline watched in horror as Lucifer gained on the boy. Closer and closer. He would catch him, for sure. She bit her lip till it turned white. Trent made it to the shallows but Lucifer was only a breath behind. She saw the Gator's mouth open to chomp on the boy. She screamed.

Suddenly, Lucifer roared with anger and twisted backwards, snapping wildly. Pirate and The King had bitten down hard on the alligator's tail. They were flung away as Lucifer's powerful tail lashed from side to side. Pirate landed hard on the bank but leapt to his feet. The King dodged Lucifer's jaws and bit a stout hind leg. Fast as lightning, Pirate darted in and bit the other. Lucifer howled with fury.

Trent made it onto to the bank and ran to where Caroline stood in safety.

There was a frenzy of spraying water, dogs and thrashing alligator in the shallows. Caroline shrieked that Trent was O.K., that they could come back. The Wolfhounds looked tiny in comparison to the giant alligator. Surely they'd be killed!

It took a few moments for her words to penetrate the dogs' fighting rage. Abruptly, The King jumped clear. As Lucifer lunged after the black dog, Pirate beat a hasty retreat. They raced up to the kids and then all four of them ran back home, away from the evil Gator. They tore into the cottage, banging the front door.

Freddie looked up from her painting. The children were a nasty shade of pale and the dogs looked inordinately pleased with themselves.

"What mischief have you all been up to?" Freddie was a little annoyed at being interrupted. "Pirate, you promised to keep them out of trouble."

"We saved the boy from ending up as Lucifer's dinner." The King snarled at her. They should be rewarded not criticized for saving that ornery pup.

"It was a grand fight, Freddie. We gave that Gator a drubbing he won't forget." Pirate bounced about with excitement. His blood still flowed strong from the fight.

"Well, I stand corrected. I beg your pardon, King." Freddie stroked the dogs' heads. "You boys did a splendid job. Did you fall in the river, Trent?"

"No, Ma'am." Trent said shamefaced, looking down at his bare feet. "Caroline told me not to go in the water but I wouldn't listen."

As the boy looked truly remorseful, and scared within an inch of his life, Freddie decided to forgo further scolding. "I presume you'll listen better next time?"

"Yes, Ma'am," he vowed fervently.

The experience took some of the wind from Trent's sails. But Mother Nature knows young boys and makes them resilient like rubber balls. He was back in true form by the next day.

They had many other adventures over the hot days of August, though none quite as exciting.

One day, with the Captain's help, they freed a Pelican who was caught on a branch. A fishing line was wrapped around his leg and the hook had gotten caught. He told them he was most grateful. The line had been there for a month. He politely offered them some fish but the Captain hastily refused and said they had plenty. The Pelican's breath smelled like rotting fish because he stored them in his pouch like bill.

A gray Persian cat, matted and thin, wandered into The Hollow late one night. He had jumped out of the car when his family moved and didn't know the way home. Sinbad, the cat, was distraught over losing his family. Trent comforted the cat with great compassion. Freddie began to understand why The Hollow had wanted him.

Esmerelda was the only one put out by Sinbad's short stay until Freddie found his family. She said she could abide almost anything but she could not abide other cats. Caroline finally understood why there was only one cat at The Hollow. Esmerelda hissed nasty things at poor Sinbad until Freddie threatened to lock her out. The tabby then stalked into the bedroom and remained there until the interloper left.

Most mornings Trent and Caroline cleaned John Henry's stable. Unless the Captain took them out on his boat. This morning, however, the Captain was out to sea.

So Trent mucked out the manure and pitched it into a wheel barrow. Then Caroline pushed the full barrow over to the mulch heap, composed of leaves, manure, leftover vegetables and coffee grinds, and dumped it. Trent pushed the last load for Caroline over to the heap. "Men do things like that for ladies," he explained, when she looked surprised. Caroline smiled at the handsome boy, feeling quite grown up.

They spread the fresh manure out to dry. Later it would be used for fertilizer. It had to be aged or it burned the plants. Freddie told them this was why the garden thrived so well.

They were both hot and sticky when they finished.

Freddie came out of the house and complimented them on a job well done.

"I think you two hard workers deserve a treat. How would you like to ride John Henry into town for ice cream sundaes?"

"Oh, yes please, Aunt Freddie!" Caroline said excitedly. They never had ice cream at The Hollow. It always melted before they got home as John Henry refused to hurry.

"You don't have any more work you need done, Miss Freddie?" Trent said, feeling he should be working for his day's wages.

"I think it can all wait till tomorrow." Freddie said and hid her smile. Trent was much improved since he'd come. So polite and responsible, and he didn't sulk so much either.

She gave them five dollars. "That should be enough for two of those disgusting banana splits with everything on them. Eat until you're sick."

Caroline and Trent laughed. Freddie often said silly things like that.

John Henry agreed to take them in exchange for a grooming. The horse adored being scratched with the spiny rubber curry comb.

Freddie gave them each a leg up onto John Henry's warm bare back. They set off to town with Pirate in the lead.

"You watch out for them, Pirate," barked The King, "I'm holding you responsible."

"I'll watch them. I promise." Pirate answered.

The children waved gaily to the cars that passed, as they jogged alongside the road to Boggy Creek.

John Henry stopped at the Post Office. He wanted to visit with Miss Mary. They could come meet him when they were ready. He would be fine, he said.

When Caroline glanced back, the horse was already standing in the shade of a blooming Magnolia. Miss Mary fed him peeled carrots one by one.

Trent grinned, when she motioned him to look. "John Henry certainly looks as if he's doing fine."

"Doesn't he always, the spoiled hayburner," said Pirate. "Are we getting ice cream, now?" The dog's tone was plaintive. His heavy fur coat was hot in the summer.

Soon the children were sitting at the Soda Fountain counter with triple scoop banana splits in front of them. Pirate swallowed his scoop whole.

The dog wanted to visit some of the town dogs and asked if the children minded.

They said no and Pirate hurried off. Caroline giggled.

"What's so funny?" Trent mumbled around a mouthful of ice cream and banana.

"He's going to see his girlfriends. Did you notice how many yards have dogs that look like him?"

Trent snickered. There certainly were plenty of tall, thin dogs in town. The Store Owner, Mr. Sweete, chuckled too. Everyone in Boggy Creek knew the handsome Wolfhound's popularity with the local ladies.

"How's your Aunt faring, Caroline?" Mr. Sweete asked.

"She's great. She just finished a new group of paintings. The Gallery Owner in the City wants her to go down for the Opening."

Mr. Sweete's eyes twinkled behind his round spectacles. "He should prepare for disappointment."

Caroline nodded in agreement.

"Why?" Trent wanted to know.

"Miss Freddie hardly leaves The Hollow and never goes further than Boggy Creek. Not once in the twelve years she's lived here." Mr. Sweete explained. "I can see why. The Hollow is a special place."

Both children nodded vigorously.

They ate every bit of their ice creams and licked their spoons. After thanking Mr. Sweete, they went to meet John Henry.

They walked along the sleepy street. Three of the town boys, a year or two older than Trent, were hanging out beneath a shady oak. They swaggered as they came over and blocked the children's way.

"Well, the witch's brat is back in town," the biggest of the boys said. He had hair that needed washing and prominent front teeth.

"Just ignore him, Trent. Maybe he'll vanish like a bad dream." Caroline kept walking.

"So is Trent your boyfriend, Caroline?" The boy jeered.

Caroline stopped, angry. "Just you shut your mouth, Buck Daniels. You are the nastiest boy."

Buck yanked her ponytail. "Caroline has a boyfriend," he sang, and his two friends joined in.

"You leave her alone." Trent shouted.

"Or what, little boy?" Buck shoved Trent hard in the chest.

"Or this." Trent leapt on the bigger boy, fists swinging. Buck's friends jumped on Trent, who shortly was receiving the worse end of the deal.

Caroline stood helplessly. She was too small to aid Trent. Suddenly, she knew what to do. "Pirate! John Henry! Help! Help!" She yelled as loudly as she could.

The big boys rubbed Trent's face in the dusty road.

There was a flash of red fur. Buck yelped and sprang away from Trent. Pirate had nipped him hard in the seat of his pants. Quicker than she could see, the dog gave the other two bullies the same treatment. The three boys ran off as fast as they could.

"I'm gonna make sure your Mother knows you did this, Buck Daniels." Caroline shouted after his departing back. Trent got up and brushed himself off. His face was smeared with dirt.

John Henry cantered up. "What's the matter?"

"You're too late, horse," Pirate said smugly, "I took care of it."

"You look rode hard and put away wet, Trent." The horse snuffled the boy's neck.

Pirate licked Trent's cheek. "I'm sorry. I should have stayed with you. I just wanted to visit the Dalmation down the street."

Trent hugged his savior and told him it was O.K.

"Can we go home?" Caroline had had enough of town.

When they told Freddie the story later, Caroline passionately declared that she hated Buck Daniels.

Freddie shook her head with disapproval. "Buck wasn't always so mean. But his Father likes his boys to be manly and that means fighting at their house. He gives them a licking himself if he thinks they're sissies. Still, I'm going to have a talk with his parents." She smiled but it was not a friendly smile. "If that doesn't work, I'll have Captain Jeff speak to his Father. Jeff can be very persuasive."

The Captain's huge size was usually enough to impress even thick-skinned blockheads like Buck's Father.

"It's one thing them calling me a witch, but I will not have you children harassed by a bunch of ignoramuses."

"Are you really a witch, Miss Freddie?" Trent asked.

Freddie rumpled his curly hair with a laugh. "Do I look like one?"

"No, Ma'am." Trent thought she was awfully pretty, even if she was old. Freddie had told him she was thirty-five.

Freddie decided that Trent needed a nap. "Even heroes take a break after battle. Best cure for being knocked about." She said, and stroked his hair fondly. He was a brave fellow, going to bat for Caroline like that.

Since she put it like that, Trent discovered he was tired. He obediently climbed into the gently swaying hammock under the oaks. Sleep claimed him in moments. A hero's smile curved on his lips.

Chapter Seven

The Hollow works its magic.

The end of summer drew close. The nights became deliciously cool once more. The garden and fruit trees overflowed with good things to eat. Corn, sweet as sugar, towered above crisp watermelons. The children ate as much as they wished.

Both Caroline and Trent were tan and healthy from good food and spending most of the day outdoors.

Freddie woke early one morning and quietly fixed herself coffee. Though she enjoyed the children visiting, an hour or two of quiet was appreciated. She had always spent most of her time alone before this unusual summer.

Pirate burst in the front door, interrupting her peace. "Mailman Bob's here, Freddie."

A telegram had arrived. Freddie opened the envelope. It was from Trent's Father, who was not a man to waste words. It read:

Miss Thompson, stop, Coming to get Trent on Friday, stop Hope he was no bother, stop, Thank you, stop Martin Landrey.

Freddie set the paper aside. Friday was only two days away.

Trent was told that his Father was coming during breakfast. The boy looked both relieved and dismayed. He was glad his Father wanted him, but he didn't want to go back to his lonely house in the City. He told Freddie so.

"But now you've been to The Hollow, things will be different." She told him. The look in her dark blue eyes was very kind.

Trent shook his head. "No, it won't. Father will still be too busy and Mrs. Grumpe will still be grouchy."

Freddie took his hand. "Have I ever lied to you? You stayed at The Hollow and were changed by the magic and your Father will be too."

"He'll never stay. He'll just pick me up and we'll go. He'll have an important Meeting or something."

"No, he won't." Freddie assured him. A soft glowing light seemed to frame her for a moment.

All of a sudden, Trent believed. "If you say so, Miss Freddie." He gave her a quick hug.

Martin Landrey came Friday morning as promised. He announced his arrival at the road by blaring the horn of his expensive car. The noise was very loud and strange in the stillness of The Hollow. Freddie told the children to wait, she would meet him. The King and Pirate accompanied her.

Trent's Father paced impatiently up and down the road. That woman, Freddie Thompson, said the driveway was hard to find but this was absurd. He wondered once more why he hadn't sent his Assistant to pick up Trent. He'd planned to, but somehow, after talking to Miss Thompson, he'd agreed to come himself. He still wasn't sure how she'd talked him into leaving Trent with her after he'd runaway like that.

Well, things were going to change. The boy needed discipline, that was all. Martin made a mental note to have his Assistant look into Military Academies. A few years in uniform would set Trent on the straight and narrow.

Freddie peered through the Crape Myrtles at Trent's Father. The man was in a dark business suit. He had to be roasting on this hot a day. Freddie wore her old shorts and a sleeveless tank top.

"It looks like we have our work cut out for us," she whispered to the dogs.

"I wonder if only a couple days at The Hollow are enough. He looks like a hard case." The King growled quietly.

"Oh, I hope it will be, dear. I'd feel terrible sending Trent back to that colder than an icebox home. Well, here goes." Freddie motioned and the bushes parted.

Martin had his back to her and she startled him when she said hello. "Glad to find you, Miss Thompson. Where did you spring from?" He asked with a smile. He admired a woman who kept her figure, it showed discipline. Martin Landrey was very big on discipline.

"It's nice to meet you, Martin. Please call me Freddie. We're very informal at The Hollow. I'm sorry but you'll have to leave your car here. My drive isn't suited to vehicles. You needn't worry, no one will bother it."

"I don't doubt that. Can't imagine you get too many strangers way back here." Privately, he couldn't imagine why anyone would live here.

"Only Trent, of course. That's how I knew he was special. Did you bring a bag?"

"For what? I'll just get Trent and be off. I have an important Meeting tomorrow."

Freddie concentrated on touching the magic as hard as she could. It was so much harder to reach adults who were set in their ways than children or the young in spirit. "But you must stay. I have my heart set on it. I thought we'd take the children canoeing. Please." She drew strength from The Hollow and wished him to stay.

Suddenly, Martin took off his jacket and tie with a grin. "Well, just see if I won't. I haven't been canoeing since I was in Boy Scouts."

"Is that so," said Freddie without inflection.

For a moment Martin felt like a heel. Maybe he should have taken Trent canoeing sometime. He ran a hand through his hair, confused. He didn't have time for such nonsense. Businessmen didn't. The boy had everything he needed after all.

Freddie went on, ignoring the rapid change of expression on his clean shaven face. "Trent is very good at canoeing and I know he is looking forward to showing you."

Pirate nosed Martin's hand. It was obvious the man needed to spend more time petting dogs. Freddie nodded to the dog, approvingly. Martin Landrey was stubborn. She decided to send a Seagull after Captain Jeff. Changing Martin would take all of their best efforts.

"Handsome dogs, you have," he commented. His hand slid down the silky coat that reminded him of the Irish Setter he'd grown up with.

"There are more of them at the house. We run long on dogs at The Hollow." Freddie chuckled. "Now we must head down to the cottage. I know Trent is eager to see you."

The two children sat by the window and watched for Trent's Father.

Trent's mouth was agape when he saw his oh-so-serious Father smile at Miss Freddie as they approached. His sleeves were rolled up and his collar open. Trent had not seen him so relaxed since Mother died.

"He looks nice." Caroline whispered, though the adults were too far away to overhear.

"It's because of Miss Freddie." Trent whispered back, feeling more hopeful. If anyone could get his Father to love him it would be Miss Freddie.

The children stepped outside to greet Trent's Father. Martin looked Trent up and down gravely. The boy certainly looked fit from hard work. Freddie had said the boy did most of the farm chores for her. He held out his hand to Trent, who shook it.

"You look well, boy," was all he said.

Caroline was astonished. "That's not how you say hello, Mr. Landrey. Parents hug and kiss their kids," she explained.

Martin looked at the dainty girl with surprise. Freddie winked and Caroline knew she had said the right thing.

"Is that so?" Martin tentatively held out his arms to his son who buried himself in his Father's firm grasp.

"Looks like the uptight stick might loosen up after all." The King growled softly.

Martin wasn't sure why everyone started laughing but the sound was contagious and he smiled too. "That big black dog of yours is a vocal fellow." Martin had heard only a growl.

"The King likes to put his two cents in." Freddie told him. "Now if we're all going canoeing I have to find you some swimming trunks. I'm sure Captain Jeff left a pair or two behind. Caroline, why don't you come help me look."

Freddie wanted Trent to have some private time with his Father.

Alone, the boy stared shyly at his Father. "I want to apologize, Sir, for running away. I won't do it again."

The lecture Martin prepared during the long drive was suddenly forgotten. "I worried about you, son. Seems you found yourself a nice spot. Freddie Thompson is a fine lady."

"She's so cool!" Trent burst out. "She paints the prettiest pictures and lets me ride her horse." He left out the fact Freddie talked to the animals. His Father would never believe it.

Martin looked at his boy carefully. A month at this place had brought back the sunny personality he'd once had. Recently all Trent did was brood in the house. For the first time, Martin realized the boy missed his Mother as much as he missed his wife. In his grief, he'd gone to work and forgotten all about Trent.

"Why don't you show me this horse you've been riding."

All the animals at The Hollow had been warned that Trent's Father needed to be dealt with carefully. John Henry waited politely in his stable. He'd grown to like Trent very much, despite their poor beginning.

Martin expected an old fat pony and was surprised to see the big, beautiful thoroughbred. John Henry pranced out, his neck arched regally, and breathed warmly on Martin's offered hand.

"Sorry, I don't have a carrot for you, you grand fellow." Martin stroked the horse's sleek neck.

"They're in the feed room," John Henry nickered helpfully.

"I'll get him a carrot, Sir." Trent always called his Father, Sir.

They fed the greedy horse several carrots.

Freddie found a bathing suit for Martin and brought towels for everyone. Caroline made a stack of peanut butter and jelly sandwiches. They were ready.

The children giggled when they saw Martin in the Captain's trunks. Trent's Father was tall but the Captain was as tall as a Basketball player. Martin made a show of tying the drawstring securely. "Wouldn't want to scare the ladies," he joked.

Freddie and Caroline giggled. Trent looked stunned then grinned, too. His Father made a joke! Maybe The Hollow's magic really was working!

They began their canoe trip upriver. Trent and his Father paddled one boat, and Freddie and Caroline another.

Freddie made sure Martin was liberally slathered with sunblock. He wasn't tan like the rest of them since he worked indoors all the time. Freddie knew it was almost impossible to work magic on someone with a bad sunburn.

The otters, Slip and Slide, were glad to see them. They performed all their favorite tricks. They slid backwards down the muddy bank and swam beneath the tipsy canoes which they rocked with nimble paws.

"Pretty cool aren't they, Sir?" Trent said shyly.

Freddie interrupted him. "Sir is much too formal for a day on the river."

Trent was aghast. His Father would be furious at Freddie for butting in. To his utter amazement, Martin smiled. "I quite agree. Shall we try Dad perhaps?"

"O.K. D-dad." Trent stumbled over the unfamiliar word. He was even more surprised when his Father risked tipping the boat to squeeze his shoulder.

"A swim would be nice," Martin said. The water was so clear and inviting. "I think I'll jump in."

"No, Dad." Trent shouted.

"What's the matter with you, boy?" Martin sounded annoyed.

"Lucifer lives around here." Trent told him.

Martin looked at his son as if he were nuts. "Are you trying to tell me the Devil lives in this river?"

Freddie hurriedly set things straight. "Lucifer is the name I gave to the very large and very unfriendly alligator who is watching us from the reeds over there." She pointed and Martin could just see the blinking eyes.

"We only swim at the Waterhole, where it's safe." Trent told him.

"Sounds like a wise idea. It seems you've learned more than a bit about the wilderness this month." Martin was pleased.

"Yes, Sir. I mean, Dad."

The canoe trip was a great success and they were all ready for a cooling dip after paddling all that way.

Freddie mentioned that the children should start picking vegetables for dinner.

"Oh, we can't be staying," said Martin.

"But you must. Captain Jeff is coming in especially to say good-bye to Trent." The Seagull brought word that the Captain was on his way.

"You can't leave," Caroline added, "the Captain always makes the best barbecues, with fish steaks this thick." She spread her thumb and index finger several inches apart.

"Please Dad," Trent pleaded, "Can't your Assistant take care of things just this once?"

Martin considered. "We can stay for dinner at any rate. I'll phone him from the car and he can take care of the paperwork for the Meeting."

"Excellent." Freddie beamed. She'd been afraid they'd leave immediately. "Trent why don't you take your Father to his car. I really wish you'd consider staying over, Martin."

The Captain's boat pulled in before Trent and his Father returned. Freddie hugged him hard. He lifted Caroline onto his broad shoulders. "So what's the problem? The Gull told me to come home, pronto."

"Oh Jeff, Thank God you're here. Trent's Father has come and he wants to send the poor boy to Military School. I've been trying but I need more magic." Freddie wrung her hands worriedly.

The Captain put a reassuring arm around her shoulders. "I'll bet you're doing just fine. You don't know your own strength."

"He called his Father, Sir. But Aunt Freddie wouldn't let him." Caroline put in.

"You don't say. Well, your Aunt is the wisest woman I know. Now, I want you to guess what kind of fish I've got in the cooler."

The magic of The Hollow seemed to be working in subtle ways. Martin returned from the car and announced that his important Meeting had been canceled. If Freddie didn't mind, he'd like to stay after all. It was the work of minutes to get the spare room set up with another bed.

Supper was delicious, as all of the Captain's barbecues were. Martin drank beers with the Captain and only looked disapproving when the dogs were each given a filet.

"You'll ruin those animals." Martin said.

The Captain chuckled and gave the smaller man a companionable slap on the shoulder. "Dogs and children are meant to be spoiled. That's why you have them. Be a poor world if all anyone did was work."

The adults stayed up late talking, long after the children went to bed.

Martin carefully stepped over his son who slept on a pad on the floor. In the soft light the boy looked younger, as he had when his Mother was alive and they had been a family. Perhaps he wouldn't send Trent away after all, he reflected. His son was a far cry from the sullen boy he'd been, before he stayed in this strange place. It might be nice to spend some time with him, maybe take him to a Football game.

With those more pleasant thoughts in mind, Martin fell asleep to the crickets' nightly chorus.

Due to the magic and all of Freddie's most persuasive arguments, Martin stayed the whole weekend. He fed fresh fish to Wavedancer, who came to visit. Trent showed him the woods and the local wild creatures. The younger dogs, who adored having visitors, didn't leave him alone for a minute though he never understood their language. The magic wasn't strong enough for that. But he did form a blossoming new bond with his son.

It was with a happier heart that Freddie said good-bye to them on Sunday. She, Caroline, the Captain, all the dogs and even John Henry and Esmerelda had walked up the drive to see them off.

"Don't be strangers to The Hollow," Freddie's eyes were moist as she hugged Trent, "Be sure to write me."

"Me too," said Caroline and hugged him as well.

"May your skies be clear and your sails never luff," was the Captain's nautical good-bye.

Trent gave a special farewell to The King and Pirate. He bent down and whispered in their soft ears. "Thank you for rescuing me. I'll never forget you."

"Just come back soon, boy." The King said gruffly. He hated anyone thinking he was sentimental.

Pirate had no such qualms and gave Trent a wet swipe with his tongue. "We'll have more adventures together. You just wait and see."

In the days that followed Caroline did miss Trent. It had been fun playing with another kid who understood the magic. But Pirate and The King were her constant companions and it was nice having her Aunt all to herself.

She was awfully glad that Trent's Father had turned out to be so kind. Aunt Freddie said he'd forgotten how to love when his wife had died, but the magic at The Hollow had taught him once more.

She wondered if her own parents would ever come. They had been gone so long. Before she went to sleep that night, Caroline wished on a star that they were all right and would come home soon.

Chapter Eight

A Trip to the City

A small sigh escaped Caroline as she and Pirate consumed ample helpings of Miss Emmeline's delicious strawberry shortcake. They'd brought Miss Emmeline some of Freddie's sweet white corn and the old lady insisted they stay for a snack.

Since her wild ride on John Henry to the hospital, Caroline had grown to know and like Miss Emmeline very much. The old lady's manner might be gruff but her heart was generous.

"What's the matter, girl?" Miss Emmeline asked. "Berries sour?"

"No, they're great." Caroline paused. "I was just wishing Aunt Freddie would go to her Art Opening in the City. It would be so much fun. The Gallery is in a fancy building on the Harbor and they'll serve lovely things to eat. Trent lives down there, too."

"Doesn't seem to me that Freddie cares much for fancy places and shindigs but I'm sure she'd like to see the boy. Why won't she go?" Miss Emmeline gave Caroline another dollop of fresh whipped cream.

"Aunt Freddie won't leave The Hollow. She says she doesn't have a car to take us and Captain Jeff will be in Port and she wants to stay with him."

"What if Jeff went with you all?" Miss Emmeline suggested.

"Then there's no one to take care of the animals at The Hollow." Caroline sighed again. Aunt Freddie had given her a long list of reasons why she absolutely could not leave The Hollow.

"I'd take care of the group at The Hollow." Miss Emmeline offered. "Been caring for livestock since I could walk. I grew up on this farm, you know. I could take Mitzi with me and stay there for a few days. My hired man can take care of my place. Nowadays he does most of the work anyhow. I'm too stiff to climb up on the tractor."

Caroline's face lit up. "If the Captain went, maybe Aunt Freddie would. Do you think he'll want to go?"

"You'll have to ask him yourself." Miss Emmeline smiled encouragingly. "Jeff has always liked a little excitement. I think you'll find he's on your side."

"I'd like to go, too." Pirate chimed in. Miss Emmeline stroked his soft ears. Since her close brush with death, the Magic had grown strong in the old woman. She chuckled. "You see Caroline, there are lots of folks on your side. You tell your Aunt I'll take care of her critters if she decides to go."

"Thank you, Miss Emmeline." Caroline said excitedly. "I've got to go. If we hurry we can catch the Captain down river before he gets to Aunt Freddie's." She took her dirty plate and Pirate's into Miss Emmeline's kitchen and set them in the sink. She brushed a quick kiss on the old lady's cheek and hurried out. Pirate, just as anxious, trotted by her side. The dog thought the City sounded glamorous just as Caroline did.

Miss Emmeline smiled as she watched the little girl and the enormous dog run across the hay field. Her weathered hand touched her cheek that still felt warm from the spontaneous kiss. "Caroline's a dear thing, isn't she, Mitzi?"

The poodle wagged her tail in agreement.

Caroline was out of breath when they finally reached the river. They had run the whole way as it was John Henry's day off. Unless there was a dire emergency, no one could persuade John Henry to give them a ride on his day off, not even Freddie. So on Thursday's, Caroline had to make do with her own two feet. She sat on the bank and Pirate flopped down beside her.

"I hope we're in time. I'd hate to have run all that way for nothing." Caroline gasped out.

"We are. I hear his boat coming." Pirate jumped up and waded into the shallows to greet the Captain when he came around the bend.

Captain Jeff readily fell in with their plan for a trip to the City. He rubbed his unshaven jaw with a delighted grin. "Sounds like a grand idea. Do you know I have never taken Freddie out anywhere but Mr. Sweete's. Not even once. Now that I think on it, I don't believe I've ever seen her wear anything but cutoffs or jeans in the winter time."

"I bet she'd look really pretty in nice clothes." Caroline hinted. The Captain was no different than any other man in enjoying his lady dressed up.

"I bet she would at that. I spruce up real pretty myself," the Captain added. Both Caroline and Pirate thought that tremendously funny and laughed until they were back at the landing.

Freddie was unmoved by either the Captain's or Caroline's pleas.

"Why would I want to leave The Hollow so I can stand around with a bunch of pretentious Art Critics who cut down my work while drinking free wine? Even if Miss Emmeline did stay at The Hollow, we have no way to get there, and if we did go, where would we stay?"

"I could take anyone who wants to go in the boat. Drop you off right at the Gallery in fact." The Captain prodded.

Freddie's thick eyebrows knit together. "No." And she left, disappearing into the woods.

The Captain bit into a crisp apple and put his feet up on the kitchen table. "Well, that might have gone better."

Caroline shook her head sadly. "We'll never get her to go." Then an idea suddenly struck her. "Captain, I've got to talk to John Henry."

"Go ahead. I'm for a nap. Now don't be too disappointed. Freddie can stick tighter than a hundred ton anchor when her mind is set."

The King was in the stable with John Henry. Caroline told them about the Opening and the idea she'd had to convince Aunt Freddie. She asked John Henry for a lift to town. The horse thought going to the City was a grand notion. He and the King had traveled widely before living at The Hollow.

"I'll take you this once." John Henry conceded. "But don't you start thinking you'll get to ride every Thursday."

Caroline solemnly swore she would not.

John Henry galloped into town. By this time Caroline was so used to riding bareback that she didn't even budge when the horse spooked sideways. John Henry mistook a stick for a snake. They went straight to Mr. Sweete's Drugstore. There was a pay phone there, so if you wanted to make a call that was where you went.

Caroline collected all the change in her pockets and deposited them in the old fashioned wall phone.

She waited while the phone rang twice then thrice. When she began to worry that no one was home, Trent's cheerful voice said hello. Quickly, Caroline explained her plan. Trent enthusiastically agreed.

"I'll ask my Father now. He's in a good mood. His Company just did another Takeover. Wait in town. It won't take long. Good thinking, Caroline." The line went dead.

Caroline hung up the phone. If this didn't work nothing would.

"You look awfully serious, Caroline." Mr. Sweete said as he polished his spectacles. "Anything I can do?"

"No, thank you." Caroline bit her lip and wondered how long it would take to get Trent's reply.

"Well then, how about a soda?"

Caroline decided there was certainly enough time for a cherry soda. She picked out a large stick of butterscotch candy for John Henry.

When she got to the Post Office a telegram was waiting. Miss Mary smiled as Caroline came in.

"Well, if this isn't good timing I don't know what is. A telegram just arrived for your Aunt. You'll save Bob a trip out to The Hollow."

Caroline carefully tucked the envelope into her pocket. Miss Mary came outside to say hello to John Henry. He blew softly into her salt and pepper curls.

Pleased that their trip was a success, John Henry trotted gaily back to The Hollow. The King was waiting for them by the Crape Myrtles.

"We all should be there when Freddie reads the telegram. It'll be harder for her to say no." The dog suggested.

"O.K.," Caroline and John Henry nodded.

The Captain was cleaning barnacles off the side of his boat while Freddie sketched quick studies of him. He grinned when he saw the earnest expression on Caroline's face. She just might be a match for her Aunt, he thought.

"You've got a telegram, Aunt Freddie." Caroline handed it over.

Freddie read the brief note. She did not look overly pleased.

"What's it say, Sweetie?" The Captain asked. Freddie gave it to him.

The Captain read the telegram aloud:

Dear Freddie, stop, Heard about your Art Opening, stop, Presume you'll stay with us and let me repay your hospitality, stop, Bring what animals you wish, stop, Martin Landrey.

The Captain winked at Caroline when Freddie wasn't looking.

"I want to go to the City." John Henry announced.

"It would be good to be on the road again." The King nosed Freddie.

"Well, it won't be the road," the Captain said. "We'll go down on the boat. As I remember Trent lives on the Harbor in one of those expensive houses. He said they have a dock. John Henry can ride on the stern deck."

"I didn't say we were going." Freddie scowled.

"Why not?" The Captain asked reasonably, undisturbed by her cross tone. "Miss Emmeline said she'd see to The Hollow. We can all berth up at Trent's house. Even John Henry. I don't see what the problem is."

"Oh please, Aunt Freddie. Trent lives so close to the Gallery we could even walk there." Caroline pleaded.

"Come on, Freddie. It'll be fun," barked Pirate.

"I despise being coerced." Freddie glared hard at the Captain and stalked off. Ace followed silently a few feet behind.

"We're going." The Captain said complacently.

"You really think so?" Caroline wondered. Her Aunt looked terribly annoyed.

"You bet. Freddie is stubborn but there isn't a selfish bone in her body."

They left at daybreak the next morning. It would take most of the day to get to Trent and Martin's house.

The King, Pirate, Ace and John Henry were the only animals who wanted to go. Sable and Maria hated to leave The Hollow worse than Freddie. Who knew how many squirrels might sneak in during their absence. Tess and Speed decided it was better to stay with Miss Emmeline and eat cake than wear a leash and go to a party. Esmerelda, horrified by the very idea of riding a boat, said she was sure they'd have a very nice time.

Even the weather was on their side. The regular afternoon thunderstorm never materialized. A true blue sky filled with puffy, cotton candy clouds seemed to blanket the world. A full pod of joyous Fins joined them for more than an hour, leaping and diving to Caroline's applause.

John Henry stood quietly so as not to rock the boat while Pirate ran back and forth on deck telling every one to look at this or that. Freddie was still put out about the trip so everyone left her to her book, with Ace at her feet. Caroline was relieved the skies were clearer than her Aunt's mood. The boat chugged steadily on as the Captain hummed, badly off-key, while they rode the small cresting waves.

Trent and Martin met them at their dock in the late afternoon. The Landreys were dressed in tennis whites and still sweaty from their game. Freddie smiled, for the first time that day, at Trent's happy face.

"Come ashore," urged Martin. He chuckled when he saw the horse. "Well, I see John Henry made it too. It's a good thing I didn't have the grass mowed this week. He'll have something to eat."

Trent hugged all the animals and Freddie. "I'm so glad you guys came. I miss The Hollow." Freddie softened and hugged him back.

Martin opened the tall french doors that looked out over the water, and beckoned them in. The three dogs bolted past him to find the bathroom for a drink. First the King, then Pirate and then Ace drank from the toilet.

Martin was serving the humans cold drinks when there was an unholy shriek down the hall. Ace raced into the room ahead of the other dogs, his eyes wide and scared.

"Freddie," he barked, "I just wanted a drink and some woman screamed at me."

"What is the matter with that woman, Trent? Is she here all the time?" The King sounded disgruntled.

Trent laughed and Martin looked mystified. Mrs. Grumpe, the housekeeper, stormed in. "Mr. Landrey, you said nothing about having to clean up after filthy animals when I took this job. I simply won't have it."

John Henry chose that moment to stick his head through the open door. "The grass is fine. Haven't eaten St. Augustine in a long time," he whickered.

Mrs. Grumpe shrieked even louder than before and dashed at John Henry with her broom. "Go away, you brute!"

John Henry shied and took off. His hooves skidded on the wooden deck. There was a loud crash when a deck chair was knocked over.

104

"Mrs. Grumpe, control yourself. These are my guests." Martin was furious, the King in his castle.

"It's bad enough taking care of a boy who messes things up as soon as I clean them. I will not stay while these flea-ridden creatures are here. Do you hear me."

Martin Landrey was very good at giving orders. He did not take them quite as well. "If you feel that way, Mrs. Grumpe, then you had better leave."

"Are you firing me?" Mrs. Grumpe said aghast.

"I suppose I am. I'll give you a month's severance pay. That should tide you over until you have another job."

"I'll be back for my check. Of all the ungrateful. . ." Mrs. Grumpe's voice trailed off as she stomped out of the room.

Freddie, the Captain and Caroline stood with their mouthes open, stunned by the display. Ace hid behind Freddie's legs. The King and Pirate took advantage of everyone's preoccupation and helped themselves to potato chips in a glass serving bowl.

"Now, where were we?" Martin, once again the perfect host, began handing out the baked cheese puffs.

Trent shared a grin with Caroline. The awful Mrs. Grumpe was truly gone!

"I'm so sorry to cause you problems, Martin." Freddie apologised, after she checked that John Henry was alright.

"Don't be. I've been meaning to replace her but she does know how to clean. Now you have to tell Trent and me about your boat trip and how you ever got that horse aboard."

They told Martin and Trent stories until it was time to get washed up and dressed for the Opening.

John Henry wanted a full bath but Caroline and Trent persuaded him to just have his stockings scrubbed. Afterwards Caroline rubbed them with cornstarch till they gleamed white as snow. Trent combed out his long tail so there was not a single tangle. Finally, John Henry was satisfied with his appearance and they were able to attend to their own grooming. The King and Pirate did not wish to be brushed, and Ace let no one but Freddie take a comb to him.

There were enough rooms in the huge house that Caroline had her own room and bath. She stayed a long time in the enormous glass box shower with marble walls and floor. It was very grand. The velvety towels were so large they draped all the way to the floor. Caroline thought this trip to the City was going to be even more fun than she'd imagined.

She put on her stylish, black and white striped, short sleeved dress. A pair of dainty black ballet slippers completed her outfit. With a quick pirouette in front of the mirror she danced out of the room and down the stairs.

The men were ready to go. Trent and Martin wore khaki pants and polo shirts in light and dark blue. Caroline grinned at the Captain in his crisp white shorts and shirt. This was the first time she had ever seen Captain Jeff in anything but swim trunks. He looked very handsome. She wondered what Aunt Freddie was going to wear.

She did not have long to wait. Freddie and Ace walked in through the door. Ace's long black hair shone midnight blue in the light. It was obvious who had the time spent on them. Freddie had washed her hair and combed it slick back. But she wore her old jeans, that were torn in the knees, and an ancient work shirt that looked as if it might disintegrate at any moment. Caroline couldn't believe it. But Captain Jeff just laughed and laughed.

"It serves me right to expect you to be anyone other than yourself." He said, and planted a kiss on Freddie's cheek.

Martin squeezed Caroline's shoulder. "Artists are always eccentric, my dear."

Freddie looked confused and rather cross at the reactions she was receiving. "Everything I'm wearing is clean. Why are you making such a fuss? Really Jeff. May we go and get this over with. You all are acting like I've got two heads or something."

"Just one very pretty one." The Captain said prudently. "Shall we go?"

The Boardwalk along the Bay was not made out of boards at all. It was a wide paved Avenue along the water's edge. Grand homes with manicured lawns and neat fences, like the Landrey's house, faced out towards the Harbor. Groups of people strolled along in the pleasant early evening air. Carriages with placid horses ambled along, as tourists pointed out the sites and took photographs. Many photos were taken of Freddie's odd bunch as they made their way along.

John Henry called out to the hard working horses. They whinnied back in greeting. One aging, grey gelding, who stepped gingerly on his right front foot, nickered anxiously. Freddie hurried over and flagged his driver down.

"You need a ride, Ma'am?" The Driver asked, openly staring at the strange group.

"Your horse is lame." Freddie pointed out.

"Oh, he's always like that. He's an old fellow. It takes him a while to work out the kinks." The Driver looked offended. He always tried to take good care of his horse, Clarence.

"Clarence says he has a stone in his shoe." Freddie persisted.

"How'd you know his name is Clarence?" The Driver was suspicious. Martin Landrey gave Freddie a sharp glance. The Captain, Caroline and Trent grinned broadly. The magic was with Freddie wherever she went.

"Because he said so," Freddie replied impatiently. "Are you going to look at that hoof or shall I?" Before the Driver could do anything, she moved over to Clarence who lifted the hurt foot obligingly. With a hoof pick she always carried in her pocket for John Henry, Freddie pried out a small pebble. Clarence sighed with relief and wuffled her damp hair in thanks.

"That should do it." Freddie told the amazed Driver.

Clarence stepped forward with an arch in his neck and a firm step.

"Why, thank you, Ma'am. You all want a lift? It's on me. I must have forgotten to check his feet before we set out."

To Caroline's disappointment, Freddie refused the offer.

"We're not going far. Thanks all the same."

"Well, you folks have a fine evening." The Driver chuckled. "I didn't know horses were so partial to roses. I'll have to buy a dozen for Clarence." He chirped to his horse and they set off back down the Boardwalk.

"What did he mean about horses and roses, Aunt Freddie?" Caroline asked. Suddenly they all realized John Henry was no longer standing with their group. The chestnut horse had his neck stretched over an ornamental fence and was eating the deep red blossoms, one after another, from a rose bush. There were only a few buds left.

"John Henry, cut that out this instant!" Freddie yelled.

The horse paid her no mind as he bit off another. After all, he thought, flowers grow back.

A slender, gray haired woman came hurrying down the garden path. "My roses! My prize-winning Kentucky Derby roses!"

There was only one perfect blossom left.

"I am so sorry." Freddie said, distraught. She turned to the Captain angrily. "I told you coming to the City was a bad idea."

The dogs moved towards Trent and Martin, away from her blast of temper.

"Stupid, greedy horse," The King muttered. "Can't stay out of trouble for five minutes."

Meanwhile, the owner of the rose bush was taking in just who had eaten her fabulous flowers. "My goodness!" She exclaimed. "What is that horse doing here?"

Caroline bravely stepped forward. After all, it was her idea that they come to the City. "I'm so sorry, Ma'am. I should have been watching John Henry. I'd forgotten how much he likes roses and yours were such beautiful ones. If it helps any, John Henry's father won the Kentucky Derby."

The woman looked dumbfounded for a moment and then a gay smile broke out on her pleasant face. "Well, I suppose it is only fitting that he should have eaten them as opposed to the Tropicana roses." She gestured to a magnificent bush of large, coral colored blossoms.

John Henry contracted his nostrils with distaste. "I only like the red ones." He eyed the last of the prize-winning blooms wistfully. Caroline was careful not to giggle.

"If you'll introduce me to all of your friends, young lady, all will be forgiven. I am Martha Bloom." She winked at Caroline. "I think I've already figured out who John Henry is."

Introductions performed, Freddie apologized once more to Mrs. Bloom. Mrs. Bloom hastened to reassure her.

"There's no milk spilt, my dear. Amanda Jaynes will finally get to win at the Fair. My Kentucky Derby's are famous, you see, in this part of the State. She can have that blue ribbon." A wide grin spread across her face. "After all, Amanda can't say her roses were eaten by the son of a Derby winner!"

"There is one flower left, Mrs. Bloom." Trent pointed out helpfully.

The woman cocked her head to one side thoughtfully and looked at John Henry. With her gardening shears she snipped off the last rose and offered it to the handsome horse. He ate it quickly but politely. He could not understand the fuss at all. They were just flowers for Heaven's sake, though they were terribly tasty ones.

Mrs. Bloom was still chuckling after they left. "Eaten by a horse in the middle of the City!" She murmured to herself. "No one will believe me when I tell them."

To Caroline's vast relief, nothing else happened on the way to the Gallery. Her Aunt wore a tight expression on her usually congenial face. Caroline thought she looked a bit forbidding. Only Martin chatted with her. The Captain steered clear as he was bound to take the brunt of her ill humor.

"Maybe it wasn't a good idea to have Aunt Freddie come down here." Caroline whispered to Trent.

"She doesn't seem to like it much. But I'm glad you came." He whispered back.

"There's the Kunst Gallery dead ahead." The Captain announced.

Arthur Kunst's Gallery was in an old warehouse that was once owned by a Sailboat Builder. The wood shiplap siding was grey and weathered unlike the newer buildings that surrounded it. Two huge, rusted anchors, that once secured fleet Clipper ships, stood on either side of the wide doorway.

Freddie marched right in, closely followed by John Henry and the three dogs. A rather pleased expression came over her stern face as she gazed at her paintings of Wavedancer so beautifully displayed and lighted.

A stocky, brown haired man, with a luxurious mustache, angrily approached them. "Madam." His voice was harsh and clipped. "Take these animals out of my Gallery immediately! This is not a barnyard!" Arthur Kunst had never met Freddie in person, though he had sold her work for several years.

Freddie laughed for the first time that day. "Art, you have been begging me for years to come to one of these absurd Openings and now that I'm here you want to kick me out."

Arthur's eyebrows lifted so high Caroline thought they'd reach his hairline. "Freddie?" He asked, flabbergasted.

"One and the same. Shall I leave or are you going to offer me one of those stingy glasses of cheap white wine?" Freddie grinned, beginning to enjoy herself.

Arthur made a quick recovery. His smile literally oozed charm. "I'll get you a glass of my special stock. You just stay right there. Please don't let that horse knock anything over."

He walked as fast as dignity would allow, into his office. With the door closed he phoned a friend of his who worked at the local newspaper. "Jim, you better head down here on the double. I've got a hot scoop for you. No, I'm not going to tell what it is. You wouldn't believe me anyway. Just get down here and bring your camera. And lots of film," he added with a laugh and hung up.

It was going to be a lucrative day. He was sure of it. Art nudged the Schnauzer asleep under his desk with his foot. "Come on, Hansel. We have company." Art grabbed a good bottle of wine, not the low grade stuff he served in quantity, on his way out.

The small, gray dog got to its feet and followed him into the public room. When he saw the Wolfhounds, Hansel went stiff. Then yapping in fury, he attacked The King!

"Hansel!" Art cried, positive that his feisty dog had signed his own death warrant.

The King neatly hopped over the small dog and nipped its hindend. With a howl, Hansel ran back to its owner. Arthur scooped it up into his arms and inspected the bitten spot. The King, thoughtfully, had not even broken the skin. Only Hansel's pride was damaged.

"It's always the little ones." Ace commented. He might be afraid of screaming women but certainly not of midget dogs.

"Where's the food, Freddie?" Pirate asked.

"I'll see you boys get something directly." Freddie looked at the Schnauzer. "Can I trust you to behave yourself, Hansel? It's terribly bad manners to attack your guests."

The Schnauzer stared at Freddie, stunned. He understood her perfectly. "I'll be good. I swear." He yelped.

"You can let him down now, Art. He'll be fine." Freddie ordered. Arthur found himself putting his dog down. Freddie looped her arm through his in a friendly fashion. "Now are you going to give me a tour of your beautiful Gallery?"

Arthur poured generous glasses of wine for the adults, told the children there were soft drinks at the bar and in a daze led Freddie off.

Trent and Caroline left Martin and the Captain deep in conversation in front of one of the largest murals. Martin wanted to purchase it for above his fireplace.

The bar was well-stocked. Trent chose root beer while Caroline had cherry cola. Delicious smelling appetizers were spread out on a long table and the children stuffed their mouths full of smoked salmon on crackers. John Henry clip-clopped over to the tray of crudites, an artistic display of raw vegetables. The horse devoured the neat stack of carrot sticks in moments and began to eat the celery, his second favorite. The three dogs, indiscriminately, ate some of everything.

The Newspaper Reporter made it over in record time, snapping photos for all he was worth. This story would make the front page of the entertainment section. Even the little girl was adorable. It would make excellent copy.

Freddie and Art were surrounded by Critics and buyers who wished to meet the outlandish Artist with the bizarre entourage.

Caroline began to relax. Aunt Freddie was actually smiling at the Critics. Martin and the Captain grew increasingly merry as they drank glasses of fine wine. They told the children to go have fun.

It didn't seem that things could go any better when she and Trent noticed a crowd gathering on the dock outside. They pushed through the pack of people to see what was happening.

A happy squeal split the air. "Caroline! Trent! Hello. Hello." Wavedancer and his entire family pod had come to the Opening! There were six dolphins in all. "Where's Freddie and the Captain?" The Fin asked. "My Mother wants to meet them."

Caroline leaned over the water to kiss Wavedancer. The Fin raised himself up to meet her halfway.

Trent ran to get Freddie, the Captain and his Father. They hurried out with a disbelieving Art in tow.

Freddie quickly kicked off her sneakers then jumped in the water to greet the Fins. The Captain joined her with a splash.

"Art." Freddie called. "Come here and meet Wavedancer. He's been the most wonderful model for my paintings!"

Art did not dive in but he did pat the Fin's head cautiously from the dock.

After that, the entire series of paintings sold one after another at hastily increased prices. Art Kunst was a good businessman and it was his job to get the best prices he could for the Artists he represented. The biggest mural was bought by Martin who insisted on paying full price though Freddie tried to give it to him.

"It's little enough," he insisted. "After what you did for Trent and me."

The rest of their trip to the City was quietly uneventful. A mellow evening with the Landreys was followed by a smooth voyage home the next morning.

Freddie smiled hugely as she stepped onto the dock at The Hollow. The four dogs who stayed behind jumped up to lick her face. Miss Emmeline waved vigorously as she walked down the path with Mitzi and Esmerelda.

"So did you all have a nice time?" Miss Emmeline asked.

Freddie looked a little sheepish but not entirely sorry as she said. "It turned out to be better than I expected. I might have been a hair grouchy."

"The Sea Hag." The Captain added with a grin.

"Why you!" But Freddie was smiling as she shook her fist at him. "Caroline, I wasn't that bad now, was I?"

"We had a fun time, Miss Emmeline." Caroline said tactfully. Her Aunt may have been a pill during the trip but that wasn't a such big deal. Caroline's Mother was crabby at least once a day.

"Well, I suppose you all ate so much you won't want a slice of my special Silver and Gold cake. It was my Grandmother's recipe."

Everyone quickly announced they had more than enough room for cake and they went up to the cottage.

As they all sat around eating the delicious yellow cake Caroline thought it was awfully nice to be back at The Hollow.

And that she would never ask Aunt Freddie to go to the City again.

Chapter Nine

Caroline has a surprise.

Freddie was worried about her brother and his wife. She feared that Esmerelda was wrong regarding their welfare. She had even started to doubt her own inner feelings. It had been over a month with no word. The birdbath was useless. She supposed she should see about enrolling Caroline in school but that meant accepting that they weren't coming back. Freddie could not do that. Not yet.

Esmerelda padded lightly into the kitchen, as Freddie drank her morning cup. The cat hopped up on the counter and lay down, her tail curled neatly around her.

"It's time for Change again," Esmerelda said.

"What now?" Freddie looked anxious. The little cat purred in sympathy.

Another telegram arrived shortly thereafter. The King brought it down to Freddie. It was postmarked from Brazil. Freddie held her breath as she tore open the envelope. It had to be good news about her brother and his wife. It just had to be!

The telegram said:

Freddie, stop, We're fine, stop, Hope you weren't too worried, stop, In the Amazon for another few days, stop, All our love to you and Caroline, stop. Matthew and Sarah, stop.

Freddie woke Caroline to tell her the marvelous news.

A week later, Caroline heard the honk of a car horn. It must be her parents! She ran up the drive as fast as her legs could carry her.

When the Crape Myrtles opened they were standing there, both her Mother and Father. They turned and saw her at that moment.

"Caroline!" They cried and ran to hug her. She was sandwiched like a slice of bologna between them. It felt so wonderful. Tears ran down her Mother's face though she smiled. The Doctor said she was so happy she had to cry.

They all tromped down the path to the cottage. Freddie was there waiting. Caroline's Father, Matthew, gave her a hug and thumped her back in a brotherly fashion. "Caroline looks great, Sis. She's been telling us what a fantastic time she's had."

"I've grown two inches." Caroline said proudly.

"We can't thank you enough, Freddie, for watching out for her so well." The Doctor said gratefully.

"It was my pleasure, Sarah. I'm going to miss her dreadfully. We all will."

"We don't have to leave right away, do we? Can't we stay a little longer," begged Caroline.

Sarah looked thoughtful, "Well you do have school, but...," then she smiled. "I can't see that a day or two will do any harm."

Caroline stared at her Mother. Something about her was different. Then she realized what it was. "Mom," she shouted, "you're not sneezing!"

"No, I'm not," Sarah agreed.

"That wild balloon trip was the best thing that could have happened to us." Matthew said.

Freddie brought out tall glasses of fresh lemonade and they all sat in the shade. Matthew got comfortable, with Caroline on his lap, then told their story.

"We were halfway across the Atlantic Ocean, and winning the race I might add, when that storm kicked up. I'll tell you now, I was as scared as I've ever been. We tried to take the balloon above it with no luck. The storm was simply too big. The winds must have been sixty or seventy miles an hour. I lashed Sarah and myself to the basket good and tight so we wouldn't fall out. We rode those winds for days. It's a good thing your Mother is so organized. We had plenty of food and water even if it was awfully difficult to eat. The wind blew it right out of our hands."

"When the winds died down we hadn't a clue where we were. The gas for the balloon was almost gone. When we saw a small valley we knew it was our best chance for a safe landing. We'd been flying over rainforest all that day. After surviving that storm I didn't want us falling out of a tree."

"They were gigantic trees, too," put in Sarah.

"Well, we got the balloon down and wandered lost for a week or so. Our supplies were running out and we wondered what we were going to do next when we ran into a group of the local natives." Matthew smiled. "They gave Sarah quite a fright at first."

"The Chief wore a necklace of bones for pity's sake, Matthew," his wife protested.

"Bird's bones." He chuckled, then went on. "When the Chief spoke Portuguese we realized we were in Brazil. Fortunately, working for the State Department gives you a smattering of different languages. I asked for a telephone and found out it was more than a two week journey through the deepest jungle just to make a call!"

"Their village made your place seem positively cosmopolitan, Freddie," Sarah added.

"I knew you were in the jungle." Caroline said, putting her cheek against her Father's. "I dreamt it."

"Did you now?" Matthew kissed his daughter. "They took us to their village and their Medicine Woman came out to greet us. She must have been a hundred years old at least. Well, she took one look at Sarah and clapped her hands twice. Three young men immediately stepped forward to do her bidding. She gave her orders and one of them went into her hut. He came out with a carved wood mug and handed it to Sarah. The old woman motioned for her to drink."

"I wasn't sure I wanted too. It smelled so awful. But we were their guests so I drank it. Within a minute or two my nose and ears cleared. It was a miracle." Sarah said passionately. "It's a tragedy that the world's rainforests are being cut down. They provide so many critical healing herbs."

"Of course we couldn't leave until we knew how to make that concoction, so it took us a while longer to get home again. And now, here we are!" Matthew gave Caroline a big kiss.

Since Sarah no longer had allergies they stayed at The Hollow for almost a week. Caroline hid her grin when her Mother pet the dogs cautiously. She might not sneeze anymore but she was still a little afraid. Sarah never could hear them but Matthew did. He had long conversations with The King every evening on the front porch.

Finally, it was time for them to go. Sarah had to return to her medical practice. Matthew to his job with the Government, and of course, Caroline had school.

The last night, when her parents went to make phone calls in town, Caroline realized the next morning they would have to go home. She couldn't bear to leave her Aunt and all the darling animals. Freddie found her in John Henry's stable crying into the horse's thick mane. The King and Pirate howled in sympathy.

"I don't want to leave," she sobbed, "Mother won't even let me have a goldfish."

"But your Mother doesn't have allergies any more," Freddie said and held out her hand. "Come with me. I have a surprise for you. I was waiting until tomorrow but I think you need it now."

Caroline took her hand and went back to the cottage with her Aunt. They went into Freddie's bedroom. In a box, behind the puffy armchair, was a tiny jet black puppy fast asleep.

"I bought this puppy for you to take back home. Her name is Sadie." Freddie whispered, not wanting to wake the puppy.

"Is she a Wolfhound?" Caroline asked.

Freddie laughed. "I wouldn't do that to your Mother. Wolfhounds need room to run or they are in trouble all the time. First time dog owners need something good-natured and well-behaved. Sadie will be like that. She's a Labrador Retriever."

This time Sadie heard her name and woke up. She looked at Caroline with lively brown eyes.

"Hello. Are you my little girl?"

When Caroline said yes, the puppy wagged her tail so hard she almost toppled over. "Pick me up. Pick me up."

Caroline did and was in love from that moment.

Sarah took the addition of a dog into her immaculate home with good grace, though she warned Matthew and Caroline they would have to care for it. But Caroline saw her Mother cooing to the puppy, when she thought no one was looking, and knew Sarah would love Sadie, too.

The next morning came all too soon. It was time to go back to the City.

All the animals were kissed good-bye. Freddie stood at the car window and hugged her niece once more. "Don't forget, Matthew. You promised me, Caroline could come back next summer."

Caroline leaned out the window and whispered in her Aunt's ear. "Will I be able to hear Sadie when I leave The Hollow?"

"Maybe not in plain English," Freddie whispered back, "but if you listen with your heart you'll always understand her. Captain Jeff sent word with the Seagull that he wishes you smooth sailing and a swift return voyage. He's so far south, he couldn't come see you off. I love you, dear. Don't be gone too long."

The car drove off and they waved good-bye.

Freddie walked back to the quiet cottage. It seemed empty with Caroline gone. The King and Pirate moped on the kitchen floor. All summer they had watched Caroline. Now they had nothing to do.

Suddenly, there was a bang on the door and John Henry stuck his head in. "Good God, you are a dreary bunch! Come on, Freddie. I'm taking you for a gallop. You look like you need the wind in your face. You dogs come, too. You'd think she was never coming back from the way you all are acting."

John Henry's practical outlook was like a fresh breeze on a muggy day.

He was right. Caroline would be back. Freddie felt her heart lift.

"Then let's go, horse." She leapt onto his bare back. "Come on hounds, you too." With a glad shout they galloped off and the dogs barked joyfully beside them.

125

THE END

Thank You For Reading...

Acknowledgments:

A special *Thank You* to my friend, *ShieAnna Powell*, for the beautiful and creative layout. And for keeping me motivated through the process. I couldn't have done it without you.

Made in the USA
Lexington, KY
11 January 2018